THI TRAFALGAR CONNECTION

THE TRAFALGAR CONNECTION

Gillian Kaye

CHIVERS
THORNDIKE

This Large Print book is published by BBC Audiobooks Ltd, Bath, England and by Thorndike Press®, Waterville, Maine, USA.

Published in 2005 in the U.K. by arrangement with Robert Hale Limited.

Published in 2005 in the U.S. by arrangement with Robert Hale Limited.

U.K. Hardcover ISBN 1–4056–3444–8 (Chivers Large Print)
U.K. Softcover ISBN 1–4056–3445–6 (Camden Large Print)
U.S. Softcover ISBN 0–7862–7938–9 (British Favorites)

The text of this Large Print edition is unabridged.
Other aspects of the book may vary from the original edition.

Set in 16 pt. New Times Roman.

Printed in Great Britain on acid-free paper.

British Library Cataloguing in Publication Data available

Library of Congress Cataloging-in-Publication Data

Kaye, Gillian.
    The Trafalgar connection / by Gillian Kaye.
       p.   cm.
    "Thorndike Press large print British favorites."—T.p. verso.
    ISBN 0–7862–7938–9 (lg. print : sc : alk. paper)
    1. Trafalgar, Battle of, 1805—Fiction. 2. Great Britain—History, Naval—19th century—Fiction. 3. Large type books. I. Title.
PR6061.A943T73 2005
823'.914—dc22   2005014971

ONE

Miss Carolyn Hadleigh sat quietly reading in the spacious drawing-room of Ferrers Court in the county of Kent. She could not be called a pretty girl, but was always described amongst those who knew her in that flat and desolate area of the Romney Marshes, as 'striking'.

She was very tall and she did not try to hide the fact, for she was not ashamed of the fine physique she had inherited from her father, Sir William Hadleigh. She was also very dark. Her hair was not quite raven black and the colour was repeated in her eyebrows and in her fine, brown eyes which confirmed her intelligence and often betrayed her sense of humour.

At that moment—a fine, spring morning in 1804—she seemed to be concentrating on her book, but the letters of Clarissa Harlowe in Richardson's story of the same name could not command her attention. One minute her thoughts would be with her brother, Robert, a midshipman somewhere aboard the *Victory* with Lord Nelson, then a few seconds later, she was wondering if she would have a visit that day from Edwin.

Mr Edwin Baillie was a young lawyer in Ashford which was the Hadleighs' nearest town and it was rare for him to pass a day without riding out to Ferrers Court to see

Carolyn. She was expecting a proposal of marriage at any day. She did not know what her reply would be and it was this dilemma which distracted her mind from the problems of the fictional Clarissa who had been commanded by her family to marry a gentleman whom she did not like.

It is not that I do not like Edwin, Carolyn was saying to herself, but is liking enough for marriage?

The question was never answered, for at that moment, the door burst open and Carolyn's mama rushed into the drawing-room waving a small, closely written piece of paper.

'Carolyn, Carolyn,' cried Lady Hadleigh. 'A letter from Robert at last and it seems to be from Sardinia or somewhere in the Mediterranean; to think that it has taken six weeks to reach us, but here it is; you read it while I go and find Lizzie and tell Ben and Lucy and if . . .' but her words were lost as she hurried up the stairs in search of Carolyn's younger sister and to tell the youngest of the Hadleigh children who were in the schoolroom with their governess, Miss Grimble.

Carolyn stood up and held the letter to her. As she walked to the window, she had tears in her eyes. Brother and sister had always been close with only a year to separate their ages; Robert was almost twenty years of age, and Carolyn, nineteen. She read the cramped writing with great eagerness.

My dear Mama, Papa and Carolyn

I expect Lizzie will be cross to be left out, but there was not the room to include all of you, I send her my fondest love, also to Ben and Lucy and, of course, Miss Grimble. It is a long time since you have heard from me, but we can only send letters when we touch land or there is a frigate bound for England. For weeks, we and our frigates have been seeking Admiral Villeneuve and the French fleet all over the Mediterranean, but they manage to give us the slip. We have found a safe anchorage in the Maddalena Islands just off the north coast of Sardinia; Maddalena itself is no more than a village of forty or fifty houses. Lord Nelson is very despondent at receiving no instructions from England and we have been cruising up and down between Sardinia and Corsica for nearly two weeks.

But the great man knows that his time will come and he is ready. He has a great flair and forcefulness as a commander, yet at the same time shows much thought and humanity for his men. He even sent to Rosas in Spain for fresh provisions and with onions and lemons in our diet, we have kept remarkably healthy and free of the scurvy.

I have learned to love and respect Lord Nelson since I joined the Victory *as a*

3

midshipman; he is a strange mixture for his height cannot be more than 5ft 2ins, and with his pale face and white hair, he looks quite fragile. As you know, he lost an arm in Tenerife in 1797 and his sleeve lies empty across his breast; he concerns himself about his health and is said to be very vain, but I think we can excuse him that after his great victory of the Nile. Since then he has become quite a hero. His nature commands the love and respect of all who serve him so we must excuse the scandal of his private life and his devotion to Lady Hamilton. It seems she is settled at Merton Place in Surrey with their little daughter, Horatia.

Enough of my lord. I must speak of my respect for Captain Hardy who is a tower of strength. He and Lord Nelson have a great trust and liking for each other and have been comrades for many years.

I continue my studies to be a lieutenant when I have the opportunity. I can manage the mathematics, but find the navigation difficult. Only God knows where I will be when I send my next letter, we must hope to confront the French fleet as soon as possible.

Lord Nelson is intent on meeting them and I know he will succeed.

Do not worry on my behalf, for I am where I wanted to be and it is an honour to serve

my country under Lord Nelson; we must keep Napoleon from our doorsteps.
              Your devoted son Robert

P.S. Is Carolyn engaged to Edwin yet?

Carolyn was smiling by the time she had finished reading the letter and turned to face an excited Lizzie who had come running into the room. The two girls would never have been taken for sisters. Carolyn was tall and dark like her father, while Lizzie resembled Lady Hadleigh in her small neat figure and her bright blue eyes, she had a mop of curly fair hair and her mama complained that she was always untidy. She was very pretty, very excitable and much loved by her family.

'Oh, please show me the letter, Carolyn,' Lizzie said. 'I thought we should never hear another word. Dear Robert. All the news we ever hear is whether the prime minister is going to resign or if poor King George has become ill again . . .' She sat down on a stool by the fireplace and Lady Hadleigh and Carolyn were entertained by a succession of 'oohs' and 'aahs' culminating in a giggle as Lizzie read the postscript.

She looked up at Carolyn. 'Are you going to marry Edwin? I shouldn't if I were you; he seems a very dull stick though I suppose that he could be considered handsome.'

'Edwin has not asked me to be his wife,

5

Lizzie,' replied Carolyn with disapproval in her tone at her sister's disparaging remark. Then she gave an inward sigh as it came to her that Lizzie was right—Edwin was a 'dull stick'. He was very serious and respectable and obviously doing well in his chosen profession, she had to admit, and he had recently purchased a considerable property and estate on the edge of Ashford.

Lizzie chose to ignore the reprimand in her sister's voice. 'I wonder how long it will be before Robert is home again?' she said. 'Is it very dangerous, Carolyn, being aboard a ship of the line?'

Carolyn was serious. 'I think the plan is for Admiral Nelson to keep the French from entering the English Channel; if the two fleets meet and there is a battle, Lizzie, then of course it will be dangerous. But we are in constant fear of Napoleon invading England; it is his intention, you know, and we rely on the navy to defend us. We must be proud of Robert; he knew the dangers when he became a midshipman—goodness gracious, it is five years ago and he was only fourteen years old, younger than you are now.'

'He will soon be twenty,' said Lizzie. 'I expect he will become a lieutenant and be very grand.'

Carolyn laughed. 'It is one step to becoming a commander or vice-admiral, I suppose. We must be proud of him, as you say and it . . .'

6

Carolyn could not finish what she was going to say about their much-loved brother, as there came a sound of a knock on the front door and then the voice of the maid admitting a visitor.

'It is Edwin,' said Lizzie. 'Shall I go?'

'No, of course not,' replied Carolyn, and to her dismay realized that she sounded snappish. 'Edwin is very fond of you; he says that you are a very pretty little miss!'

Lizzie wrinkled her face in a frown. 'I would rather be tall and handsome like you, Carolyn. You are much admired, but people always think of me as a "pretty little thing".'

Carolyn smiled. 'I think that you will grow into being a fair beauty one day, Lizzie, you take after Mama and she must have been beautiful when she was young. She still is now, I suppose, and she has great dignity.'

Lizzie sighed and then gave a smile as Edwin came into the room. 'Hello, Edwin,' she said and added, quite without thinking, 'Do you want to be on your own with Carolyn or shall I act as a chaperon? Can one be a chaperon at sixteen, I wonder?'

Edwin made a formal bow to them both, then spoke to Carolyn, ignoring Lizzie's remark. 'It is a fine morning, my dear, shall we take a walk and leave Lizzie to amuse herself?'

Mr Edwin Baillie was not a tall man, he looked down on Carolyn by only a few inches, but he was slenderly built and elegant, with light-brown hair brushed fashionably forward.

7

He was not the dandy, his waistcoat was always plain and he was inclined to dark colours. That morning, his breeches were grey and his coat a shade darker, his neckcloth faultless.

He was generally regarded as a serious young gentleman and was much admired by the young ladies of Ashford. However, it was to Ferrers Court he looked for his choice of bride, for he had decided that Miss Carolyn Hadleigh would suit him very nicely. He could not say that he loved her, but he admired her and considered that she would grace the hearth of his new home in Ashford very well. He also knew that Sir William Hadleigh was a wealthy man. He gave Carolyn his attention as Lizzie left the room.

'You are not dressed for riding today, Edwin,' Carolyn was saying. She was used to riding out every day and Edwin often accompanied her.

'No, I have brought the tilbury. I wish to talk to you seriously and it is hardly possible to do that when we ride together.'

Thoughts of a proposal once again surfaced in Carolyn's mind and she tried to dismiss them as she went upstairs to fetch her pelisse and bonnet.

Ferrers Court was a low rambling house not far from the small village of Aldington and on the edge of the Romney Marsh proper. The land around the house was flat, well-drained and very fertile.

Carolyn had loved its vastness, the low horizon across the Marsh and the distant prospect of the sea for as long as she could remember, but Edwin considered it dull and always preferred to make his way upwards to the villages of Wye and Hastingleigh on the downs of east Kent. It was beautiful countryside and its lanes were more sympathetic to the wheels of the curricles and gigs than were the narrow rough tracks across the Marsh.

They drove in silence for a long time until Edwin reined in on the brow of a hill as they approached Hastingleigh; there was a lovely view across the River Stour and in the distance the Marsh stretched endlessly towards the sea.

'I always like it here,' Edwin remarked. 'I discovered it soon after moving to Ashford and I like to return from time to time.'

Carolyn looked at him, but his expression gave nothing away. In many ways, he was a mystery to her as he spoke little of his family who, he had told her, had been wealthy landowners in the north-east of the country before settling themselves in London. Sometimes his reticence made her feel uneasy.

He turned to her and gave a slight smile. 'Carolyn, I have brought you here for a purpose. I have known you now for nearly a year and during that time I have been able to purchase Ridley House near Ashford and the land that goes with it. I bought it with you in mind, for I have a great admiration both for your looks and your good sense. The time has come for me to do you the honour of asking you to become my wife. In other words, I am asking you to marry me. I know that I should have approached your father first, but I do not consider myself to be a young tearaway and I am sure that Sir William would approve of my profession and standing in Ashford; I think he would also applaud my purchase of Ridley House. I await your reply, my dear, and I think that I know what it will be for you have never spurned my attentions. Are you going to make me a happy man, Carolyn?'

Carolyn sat immobile, staring straight ahead; she felt as though she could not move and she seemed to be unable to think coherently.

Here was a fine chance for her, she might never have a more advantageous offer. But how cold he had sounded, with no words of love or even of affection—only admiration. Am I being wicked in wishing he had tried to kiss me, she was asking herself? I would have known then if there was a true feeling between us; now there are only doubts, even suspicions.

He is certainly a fine gentleman and everyone I know of my acquaintance would consider it to be a good match. Why do I hesitate? What is it that does not ring true about him? I suppose I am being foolish because I wanted to be told that I was loved. Is there any young lady who does not dream of love? Even Clarissa loved the dreadful Robert Lovelace in the story I am reading; perhaps it comes only in such stories.

'Well, Carolyn, have you considered?'

The cold remark brought her to her senses. She was determined to be polite. 'Thank you, Edwin, for your very kind offer. I feel honoured. Would you kindly allow me a few days to think it over before I give you my reply?'

'Of course, of course,' he replied. He did not look at her and she thought that she sensed a note of testiness in his voice. 'I will speak with your father, I have no doubt that he will approve of my suit and will make a generous settlement.'

Settlement? Settlement? The word echoed in Carolyn's head. Was Edwin wanting to marry her only because he knew that her father was wealthy?

There came a sudden change in Edwin. It was as though he had steeled himself to make the proposal and now that it was done, he could rest easily and wait for Carolyn's reply.

'Give me your hands, Carolyn,' he said, as he turned to her with a smile.

She met his eyes and was thankful to find the friendly, approachable Edwin she had ridden with and danced with during the previous months. She put out a hand to find it grasped warmly in his.

'I shall await your reply impatiently,' he told her. 'I think I know what it will be and I will be the happiest gentleman in all Kent.'

'I have not agreed to marry you, Edwin,' she replied, and once again found herself waiting for the embrace which would help her to make up her mind.

Edwin was happy and cheerful and talkative as they drove back to Ferrers Court where he sought out Carolyn's father and Carolyn herself talked to her mama in the drawing-room.

'You are looking worried, my dear,' said Lady Hadleigh. 'Has Edwin said something to upset you?'

'He has asked me to marry him.'

Lady Hadleigh tried not to smile at her daughter's glum remark, but she spoke lightly. 'Your first proposal, Carolyn, and from such a respectable young gentleman.'

It was the word respectable which fuelled Carolyn's wrath, for there was certainly anger in her voice as she made her reply. 'Mama, he made it sound like a business settlement. He was so formal. Was I wrong to expect words of love or even some affection? I could not say yes to him. Am I wrong to be thinking of love, Mama? You tell me. Did you love Papa when you were married?'

Lady Hadleigh smiled. 'Our marriage had been arranged by our families, which was the custom in those days. This war with France seems to have changed things and there is not so much formality in our manners as there used to be. It does not mean to say that I was not fond of William, we had been close all our lives and we have been very comfortable together. I think love grows, Carolyn; it is wrong to expect the romance of the novels of Mrs Radcliffe which Lizzie reads. I do not think that life can ever be as exciting as that, but it does not mean to say that you would not be happy with someone like Edwin. Where is he now? I see the gig is still outside.'

'He is asking Papa's permission to marry me. I am surprised that he did not do that first. Edwin is very proper.'

Lady Hadleigh did laugh then. 'I declare that you are expecting some dashing hero to come along so that you can fall in love with him! But I cannot advise you, Carolyn dear, except to say that your father and I both feel that Edwin would be eminently suitable as a husband . . .' She stopped what she was saying as Carolyn got up and walked to the door. 'Where are you going?'

'I am going to ride on the Marsh,' said Carolyn abruptly.

'You are . . .?' Lady Hadleigh was almost speechless. 'But what about Edwin? What shall I say to him?'

'You can thank him for offering for me and tell him that I am thinking it over.'

'Very well,' replied her mama. 'Perhaps you

are wise.'

She heard Carolyn run upstairs to change into her riding-dress and then go out to the stables for Trixie, her favourite mare.

Then Edwin appeared and did not seem in the least disappointed that Carolyn was not there; he left immediately.

As she watched the gig disappear down the long drive, Lady Hadleigh was not surprised to be joined by her husband.

'Where is Carolyn?' he asked.

'She has gone riding on the Marsh; I think she wanted to be on her own. What do you think of Mr Edwin Baillie's offer, William? Will he do for Carolyn? He seems to be a very pleasant young gentleman, but I have the feeling that Carolyn is hoping for someone a little more dashing.'

Sir William did not reply immediately; he walked to the window and looked out on the land that was his. He not only owned Ferrers Court and the valuable estate which went with it, he had inherited an immense double fortune from his own father and from an uncle who had died childless.

He turned and looked at his wife. 'Do you approve of the match, my dear?' he asked.

There was something in his tone which told her that he was expecting an honest reply. She gave it. 'I cannot fault him, William. He is excessively polite to me, but always pleasantly so. He has been coming here for nearly a year

14

now and I am sure that his devotion to Carolyn is genuine. I believe he would make her an excellent husband. Why did you ask in such a way?'

He frowned slightly and came to sit opposite her across the fireplace. 'What do you mean by "such a way"? I was only hoping for your honest opinion.'

She shook her head. 'I am not sure. I thought I heard a note of doubt in your voice, a suspicion that something was not quite as it should be.'

He leaned across the hearth and took her hand in his. 'You know me, my dear.'

She laughed then, for he looked so serious. 'I should think so, too. We have been married for over twenty years and we knew each other for a long time before that. I suppose that I must be able to sense your every word and mood.'

He pressed her hand and sat back in his chair. 'You are quite right, of course. I cannot fault Mr Edwin Baillie; his manner and his dress are irreproachable; he is highly thought of in Ashford and he seems to have a genuine regard for Carolyn. I cannot call it love for I consider it an over-rated term and not entirely necessary for a successful marriage.' He paused.

'So what is it?' she asked him.

'I am not sure. It is just some uneasy instinct I seem to have.' He replied slowly as though his thoughts were elsewhere.

'That is not like you,' his wife said.

'No, perhaps not, but in Mr Edwin Baillie's case, one or two things have given me doubts. I daresay that I am being foolish for a more amiable gentleman one could not hope to have for a son-in-law.'

'He has given you cause to doubt him?' she asked next.

'It sounds foolish now I come to tell you about it, especially when I have to remember that he was very open with me. He told me that his position in Ashford was assured and that he could offer a good home to Carolyn at Ridley House; it is just outside the town, as you know, and he tells me that it will be completely refurbished as it has lain empty for some time.'

'William, do stop prevaricating. What is it about Edwin that has given you cause to doubt him?'

'Three things. He said nothing about his family for a start, though I believe that the Baillies are a respectable family from the north-east. Then I began to wonder how a young lawyer had found enough money to purchase a house and estate such as Ridley House, and . . .' He stopped as though he himself doubted his next thoughts. 'He seemed to want to know what settlements I was going to make for Carolyn; I do not think he should have asked me such a thing.'

But his wife disagreed. 'It was all very right and proper of him. He wanted to let us know that he would provide for Carolyn in the way to which she was accustomed. I think that you are worrying unnecessarily. I have a high regard for Edwin and I think that Carolyn will do well to accept him. But she is not at all sure, you know.'

'She is not?' He raised his eyebrows. 'Interesting. I will not worry about it all, we will see what time will bring. And now, shall we forget about Edwin Baillie and have another look at Robert's letter? It is so good to have news of the boy.'

While this conversation between her parents had been taking place, Carolyn had gone up to her bedroom to change ready for riding out, but she had been delayed by Lizzie who had come chasing after her full of curiosity.

'Carolyn, Edwin is in the library with Papa. Does it mean that he is asking for your hand? Are you going to marry him, and if you have accepted him, can I be a bridesmaid?'

Carolyn was in no mood for Lizzie's ecstasies, but spoke kindly. 'Lizzie, I have not turned Edwin down, but I did tell him that I would think about his proposal. I cannot wait to be out of the house and on my own, so while I get into my riding clothes, would you please run down to the stables and ask Barny to saddle Trixie for me.'

17

Lizzie stared. 'You are never going to ride out on the Marsh when you have only just received a proposal of marriage?'

'Yes, I am. I can think better when I am on the Marsh,' replied Carolyn, struggling to do up the many buttons of her riding coat. She had always shocked her family by wearing an old pair of breeches of Robert's and a hunting jacket when she rode on her own. On these occasions, she did not use a side-saddle as she did when riding with Lizzie or Edwin, and the neighbourhood had become accustomed to seeing her heading for Romney Marsh as though she was a boy.

'Are you going to run to the stables for me, Lizzie?' she asked, as she struggled into her riding boots.

Lizzie knew her sister in this mood. 'Yes, yes, of course, and you don't mean the side-saddle, do you?'

'No, of course I don't,' snapped Carolyn. 'Why do you think I am in breeches and riding boots? Please go.'

'I've gone,' said Lizzie, and ran out of the door, leaving Carolyn hunting for her old leather gloves. Within minutes, she was running down the stairs and she reached the stables just as Barny, the stable boy, was putting the saddle on Trixie and fastening the girth. He was used to Miss Carolyn's ways and touched his cap as she jumped into the saddle and rode off in the direction of the Marsh.

18

TWO

Romney Marsh beckoned Carolyn; it had always been so. Not for her the beauties of the Downs, it was the Marsh which called her. The mysterious no-man's land of ditches and dykes where even the willows struggled to survive the winds of the not so distant sea. There were few villages and the sheep outnumbered the people dwelling in that very special part of Kent. The men of Romney Marsh had long governed themselves; they had their own unique and very ancient local system of government known as the Lords of the Level.

Carolyn was especially conscious of her heritage and beyond their own village of Aldington, she knew every narrow lane and every track. She knew where to find a welcome at an isolated farmhouse and she particularly welcomed the sight of the ancient church of Newchurch. It was by no means as new as its name suggested having been built and used since the thirteenth or fourteenth century. It was a tiny village and she usually made it her goal when she rode on the Marsh. Here she was within a few miles of the sea and liked to think that she could feel the salt spray in the air.

That day, she jumped on Trixie without any help from Barny or from Lizzie who was still standing there. She rode through their own village of Aldington without even noticing it— her mind was on Edwin and on Edwin's proposal.

Out of the village, she was on the Marsh proper and she slowed down; it was not a place to hurry. The water lay unruffled in the long straight dykes, the mist lingered over the willows, even the grazing sheep seemed motionless. Time hung in the air.

On a straight lane out of Aldington which was little more than a cart track, she walked Trixie carefully, but her horse, from instinct, seemed to know where the stones lay and never faltered.

Carolyn paused at a gate and gave a deep sigh; sometimes the wind off the sea was keen and cold, but that day she was glad of the stillness of the scene. Edwin does not like it here, she was thinking, that alone should tell me something, but if I married him, I would not lose the Marsh for we would be settled in Ashford. Then I must consider that I will soon be twenty years of age and living in such an isolated place, what chance do I have of meeting any gentleman who would be considered as eligible as Edwin?

She watched the mist move slowly over the edge of the nearest dyke, the sheep moving among the rich grass of the marshland almost without a sound. In the distance, she could see what appeared to be a low barn, but Carolyn knew it to be the cottage of old Granny Harland. Always known as 'Granny Harland', she was a great age, a widow, who lived with her grandson, Joel, who was a 'looker' on the Marsh. In the dialect of the Romney Marsh, a shepherd was known as a looker.

Granny will have some words of sense, thought Carolyn, and rode off along twisting tracks until she reached the cottage; she and Robert had often ridden here on their ponies to be given teacakes or fresh crusty bread straight from the oven. Granny Harland baked every day for her large family which consisted of Joel and his wife, Mary, and their six children.

As Carolyn approached the squat building, she saw some of the children playing with an old wheel from a cart; the older ones would be off with Joel, learning the ways of the Romney Marsh sheep. She had remembered to put some coins in her pocket and gave each of the children a penny piece for looking after Trixie for her; they would be able to spend it in the small shop in Newchurch.

The combined good smells of newly baked bread and onions and herbs from the stew-pot welcomed her as she went in the door. Joel's wife was suckling their new baby in the front room and Granny Harland appeared in the doorway of the kitchen as soon as she heard voices.

There were no bedrooms in this humble

cottage; a ladder took them up to the roof space under the thatch where they all slept on straw mattresses. Plain living, plain food and the Harland family were rarely ill.

Carolyn had a word with Mary Harland before going up to give Granny a kiss.

'Hello, Granny Harland,' she said, as she smiled at the old lady. 'Can I come and talk to you?'

'Miss Car'lyn.' Granny never could get her tongue round Carolyn's name. 'You know as you is welcome any time. Come in the kitchen. Will you have a glass of milk or p'raps you'd rather have some small ale. We've got a barrel on the go, Joel's that keen on his brewing.'

'I'll have some milk, thank you, Granny,' replied Carolyn, as she sat down at the scrubbed kitchen table. The range was in the kitchen and had double ovens; there was a wooden table and some chairs and a tall dresser which held all they possessed in the way of plates and cups, pots and pans. It was warm and comfortable and Carolyn always liked to come here.

'Sit you down then, miss, and you can tell Granny Harland all your troubles, for I'm sure that's why you've come. Not that I mind though, you musn't think that, you'm welcome any time, good or bad. And how's your Robert? Have you had any news? These is worrying times with them Frenchies only a stone's throw across the Channel and people running from their homes along the coast every time there's a rumour of invasion, but we've got the militia and them Martello towers, as they call them, to defend us, so we must trust in the good Lord.'

Carolyn was sipping the milk and listening with pleasure to Granny, a hardy woman of over sixty years of age and valued for her kindness and her wisdom. She had met with happiness and sorrow in a life when many children died in their infancy, and what they called the Marsh ague could take a man in his prime.

Carolyn was about to tell Granny about Robert when she realized with some astonishment that it was on this same day that she had joyfully read his letter, received a proposal of marriage and then sought wisdom from the Marsh and from Granny Harland.

'We had a letter just this morning, Granny, it took six weeks to get here. He was somewhere near Italy when he sent it, but there's no knowing where he might be now.'

'Well, he's with that there Lord Nelson so he should be all right, praise the Lord. So you've brought your troubles to Granny Harland, Miss Car'lyn? Last I heard, that Mr Baillie, lawyer from Ashford I believe, were a-courting you.'

'However did you know that?' asked Carolyn, but she could guess.

'All bits o' gossip come my way, miss, I'll

23

have you know. What's known in Ashford, is known in Newchurch and soon finds its way out here. You aren't my only visitor, folks is always welcome at Granny Harland's. It's nice for Mary, too, for Joel is gone from dawn till dusk and some nights we don't see him at all. There's one or two small barns on the Marsh where he can bed down. So am I right? Is it this Mr Baillie?'

Carolyn nodded. 'Yes, it is, Granny. He has asked me to marry him. Only this morning, it was.'

'You didn't accept him then?'

'How did you know?' Carolyn asked.

Granny Harland gave a chuckle. 'You'd'a been at home having an engagement party or such like, not riding across the Marsh to see me.'

Carolyn smiled. 'You are always right. I don't know why I am hesitating, Granny. I know that Edwin would make me a good husband and provide me with a fine home. He is quite handsome, too, in a quiet kind of way. Mama thinks that it would be a good marriage and I respect her opinion. What do you think, Granny Harland?'

Granny leaned forward in her chair; her old skin was brown and wrinkled, but her eyes were alight with interest and wisdom. 'I'll tell you two things for certain, Miss Car'lyn, and you'll think as them's opposites. But one of 'em speaks from the heart and one from the

24

head and it's up to you whether you follow your head or your heart.'

'Yes, Granny.'

'Head first then. There's many a fine young gentleman as would make you a good husband and be kind to you and you would have a nice family and it'd be a happy marriage. Only your head and your common sense can tell you if this Mr Baillie is the right one; he doesn't sound a bad catch to me, as the saying goes. There's another saying, too, around here at any rate; "There's as good fish in the sea as ever came out of it". Can you make sense of that?'

'I think so. If I decide that Edwin is not to be the one for me then someone else would be sure to suit me just as well. But about the heart, Granny, do you mean love?'

'I do then. You could walk out of here and see a fine gentleman riding by and you could look at him and your heart would tell you that he was the one for you.'

Carolyn laughed merrily. 'As though that could ever happen! But I know what you mean and I will remember what you say. What about you and Grandad Harland? How did you meet him? Did you love him as soon as you saw him?'

It was Granny's turn to laugh. 'Oh, Miss Car'lyn, you must realize that love can be the stuff of them fairy-tales. Life's not always like that. I was a kitchen maid in the big house at

25

Newchurch and Isaac, he were stable boy. We had the same afternoons off and we went for walks over the Marsh; we did like each other and when he was made assistant-coachman, well, we thought we would wed and we did. Never regretted it, neither. But it weren't one of them falling-in-love occasions, it were a steady courtship and a happy marriage and now I've got Joel to prove it. He's a good lad to his old granny.'

'I knew you would help me and you have. I will think about it all in a sensible fashion and I will come and tell you what I decide. My heart is not telling me that it is the right thing, Granny, but I will listen to my head and hope to come to the right decision.'

'You haven't brought him to see me,' observed Granny.

Carolyn shook her head. 'No, Edwin is from London, he does not care for the Marsh, and you know that the Marsh is very special to me. It is where I want to be when I am happy, it is where I want to do my thinking and it seems to belong to me. Do you understand, Granny?'

The old lady nodded.

'We are a bit special, us Marsh people. That's why you can come and talk to me, Miss Car'lyn, and mind you come again when you've made up your mind, or when you've had another letter from Mr Robert, the good Lord spare him and all who fight to keep this island free.'

Carolyn rode home quickly and thoughtfully. No, she told herself, my heart has not been stirred by Edwin's attentions, but my head is telling me that his is as good an offer as I can expect. I will dwell upon it for a little while until I make up my mind.

For a few weeks, all their attentions were taken up by the affairs of the country; King George slowly recovered from his derangement and his illness, and then Mr Pitt rose in the House to focus their thoughts on the situation the country found itself in, with the ever present threat of invasion across the Channel by Napoleon. His speech made a stir and it was rumoured that Addington would resign as Prime Minister.

At Ferrers Court, Sir William solemnly quoted Pitt's words to his wife and to Carolyn who was awaiting Edwin's arrival. *'We are come to a new era in the history of nations; we are called to struggle for the destiny, not of this country alone but of the civilised world. We must remember that it is not only for ourselves that we submit to unexampled privations. We have for ourselves the great duty of self-preservation to perform; but the duty of the people of England now is of a nobler and higher order . . .'*

Edwin arrived as Sir William finished speaking and was given the newspaper to read for himself.

He nodded sagaciously. 'We need Pitt at the helm,' he said. 'You mark my words,

Addington will resign within days.' He turned to Carolyn. 'Shall we take a walk in the grounds, my dear? It is a sunny morning.'

Walking at his side towards the small wood which sheltered the house from the winds off the sea, Carolyn found that Edwin was enthusiastic in his support for Pitt.

'I know that Pitt is ageing,' he was saying, his tone serious, 'and he does not enjoy the best of health, but he would soon turn his attention to the defence of our island and in particular to the defences along the Channel coast of Kent. We are too near to Calais and Boulogne for comfort, I have heard rumours that Napoleon is amassing a fleet of barges at Boulogne. It is ominous news when our fleet is in the Mediterranean.'

'You are keen on politics, Edwin?' Carolyn observed.

He nodded. 'I have often had it in mind to enter Parliament, but I believe you need to be a man of some substance to do that. I am happy as a lawyer and especially so with the thought of living in Ashford with you as my wife. You will have noticed how patient I have been, Carolyn?'

Edwin's political outburst had intrigued Carolyn as she had always found him rather dull. She herself was of a lively mind and often discussed the affairs of the nation with her father; she had always felt that Sir William missed the company of his son and she did her best to make up for it.

She felt that she should make a reasonable reply to Edwin. 'I know that I have hesitated,' she said slowly. 'It is a big decision to make.'

He was silent for a few moments as they entered the wood; the trees were showing their first soft green leaves of spring and where the sun filtered through, the effect was of lightness and a lifting of spirits.

'I do love you, Carolyn.'

She looked at him, startled. Why had he suddenly told her so? Why had there been no words of love when he had first asked her all those weeks ago? She could not explain it to herself and felt suspicious. It would have been more natural in a young gentleman to declare his love first and then to have asked for the young lady's hand in marriage.

'You did not say so before,' her tone was defensive.

'I was not sure that I was acting correctly in asking you to marry me when I had not spoken to your father.'

'You are very correct, Edwin,' she said, still doubtful.

'Would you have preferred kisses and embraces, Carolyn? I am surprised at you. I am no rake and I thought that you would prefer correct behaviour.'

'Yes, yes . . .' she started to say, then stopped because he had taken her hand and turned her to face him.

'Allow me to kiss you, my dearest Carolyn,' he murmured.

'Edwin . . .'

'No protests,' he said, and she felt his lips softly on her cheek before they found her mouth. It was a long kiss, but Edwin was not rough and Carolyn found that her senses were not disturbed.

But it had been pleasant to be held close to him and to sense his consideration for her feelings. Perhaps it has told me what my answer to him is to be, she was thinking as she drew away from him.

'Edwin . . .' she started to say. He was smiling at her and the smile gave her confidence. 'Edwin, I cannot be sure that I love you, but I do like you very much. I thank you for your offer of marriage which I am pleased to accept. There, I am being very proper now . . . Edwin—' She broke off as she was caught fiercely against him and this time there was no consideration for any delicate feelings on her part.

The kiss was both rough and passionate and Carolyn could sense in him a strong feeling of triumph, a victory at having won her for himself; it was not a feeling which told her of any loving tenderness.

She felt a sense of hesitation, a wish that she had not committed herself, but it was too late. Edwin was fired with an enthusiasm she had not suspected he possessed and he kissed her again before starting to speak of the plans they could make.

'How soon can we be married, Carolyn? I hope that you are not going to make me wait too long.'

They continued walking along the woodland path and she felt troubled; she had an instinctive feeling that Edwin was not going to like what she was going to say in reply to his question.

'I do not wish to be married until Robert is safely home again,' she told him.

She felt a tenseness in his body, for he was now holding her hand. 'Wait until Robert comes home? Whatever do you mean? We have no idea what the outcome is going to be with Napoleon and the fleet must always be ready. It could be months and months, over a year, maybe.'

'I am prepared to wait,' she said calmly. 'I am not yet twenty and I will not marry anyone until I know that Robert is safe and well.'

'It is preposterous,' he spluttered. 'You have your father's blessing. You know I love you and I have bought Ridley House all ready for its new mistress; it does need refurbishing, but I know that you will enjoy doing that.'

'Were you so sure that I would agree to marry you?' she asked him. She was puzzled at his tone and his objections.

'My dear Carolyn, I have known you for almost a year and we have seen each other nearly every day. Why is there any need to wait?'

Carolyn could be stubborn when she chose. 'Why is there any need to rush?' she asked him in return. 'I will cry off straight away if you so wish and you can find another young lady in Ashford who would oblige you.'

She watched as the expression on his face changed from one of frustrated annoyance to the usual charm she had come to know so well.

'No, no, of course I do not wish for that. I am so delighted at your acceptance of my proposal that I suppose that I am disappointed that you will not name a day. Shall we go and tell your parents, Carolyn? I think they will both of them be pleased.'

She walked quietly through the trees with him knowing that he spoke the truth; her parents *would* be pleased and it gave her some satisfaction that she would be behaving as they wished. For herself, she felt contented enough with a strange feeling of being settled. Her future was assured, her husband would be a gentleman of substance and respectability and she would not be moving away from the Marsh. It is head over heart, just as Granny Harland said, she thought. I have chosen Edwin with my head and I must be contented.

The summer months of 1804 slipped past. As Edwin had predicted, Pitt became Prime Minister on 7 May and on the day that he resumed his seat as the country's leader, Napoleon was declared Emperor of the French.

During those months, Carolyn found herself faring very well with Edwin. Since discovering his interest in politics, they found themselves with absorbing discussions on Pitt's plans to strengthen the army and the defences. Edwin was of the opinion that the Prime Minister planned to take the war to the French rather than sit and wait for the expected invasion of English soil.

Then they learned the news of the building of a canal across Romney Marsh; it was to be called the Royal Military Canal and linked the River Rother to the River Rye. It was to stretch right across the Marsh and was to be Pitt's scheme of defence along the coast in connection with the Martello towers. The round squat towers had been built all along the Channel and the German Ocean coast from Sussex to Suffolk and each held a 24-pounder long gun.

There was a tower at Dymchurch on the edge of the Marsh and when Edwin learned of the plans for the canal, he was keen to see it being constructed.

Carolyn was delighted, thinking that at last she would get Edwin on to the Marsh.

We can ride over the Marsh to Ruckinge,' she told him. 'Papa says that the canal will pass quite close; Ruckinge is on higher ground just there and will overlook the canal.'

But Edwin had other ideas. 'There is not a road across the Marsh as you know, Carolyn, and I will want to use the gig. We will take the road from Ashford to Hythe and then out to the village of Saltwood, for I read that the canal starts very close to that village.'

Carolyn sighed, but had to agree; perhaps, in a way, it would be better to keep the secrets of the Marsh to herself, even after she was married to Edwin.

It turned out to be a very successful and harmonious trip. Edwin had been right in his conjecture that they would be able to see the digging going on near Saltwood and when they reached the spot, Carolyn was astonished at the great number of labouring men involved in the task. The Redcoats seemed to be directing operations.

'But, Edwin, everywhere they dig, the ground immediately fills with water.'

He laughed and laughed. 'Are you surprised, my dearest girl? The land around here is only protected from the sea by the walls and embankments; your precious Marsh is only fertile because it so well-drained by the dykes and water-courses.'

She smiled. 'Yes, I do know all that and in the past, we have had many floods. I should not be so surprised, and you are right to laugh at me. I wonder how long it will take to complete the canal? I hope that Napoleon does not get here first!'

'Our navy is superior to the French navy and will protect us in the Channel, have no fear. You are a strange girl, Carolyn.'

She looked at him in astonishment. 'Why ever do you say that?'

He considered. 'I think that most young ladies would want to be taken to Tunbridge Wells to buy muslin or whatever you call it to make a new gown. You are content to come here and watch a canal being built.'

'Perhaps you have a lot to learn about me, Edwin,' she replied; she felt at ease with him that day.

'The sooner we are married the better then. Have you changed your mind about the date of our wedding?'

She shook her head, not wanting a disagreement. 'From what news we can glean from the paper, Lord Nelson is still chasing the French fleet around the Mediterranean, but we have had no word from Robert. I have no doubt that he is safe and I expect we will have a letter before the end of the year. Perhaps the spring of next year would be nice for a wedding.'

They were sitting in the gig and Edwin's arm crept around Carolyn's waist in a rare gesture.

'Thank you, Carolyn, for those words. I could wish it might be sooner, but that is only six months away. I daresay it will all work out for the best.'

Carolyn thought this a strange remark, but made no comment and they were soon driving back along the road to Ashford.

*   *   *

But by the spring of 1805, no word had come from Robert, and Carolyn was still refusing to marry Edwin. Then *The Times* was reporting that Admiral Villeneuve and the French fleet had sailed for the West Indies and that Lord Nelson was giving chase across the Atlantic.

Yet again, Carolyn refused to name a day for their wedding. Then a few weeks later, the Hadleigh family had the joy of a letter from their eldest son.

THREE

Carolyn was out when Robert's next letter arrived; Edwin was not with her and she had enjoyed a good gallop across the Marsh which was in one of its lighter moods. The sun was pale behind a thin layer of cloud, but when it broke through, she could feel its heat for it was almost Midsummer's Day.

She walked slowly from the stables to the house feeling cheered by her ride, and, she had to confess it to herself, glad to be on her own with no Edwin at her side. They had not disagreed and he was assiduous in his attentions to her, but she forever felt the vexed question of the date of their marriage hanging over them. She was still adamant that she would not marry until Robert was safely home again.

At the house, she found her mother in a great state of excitement. 'A letter from Robert at last, Carolyn. We have all read it and Miss Grimble read it to Ben and Lucy; your father has it in the library, we could hardly wait for you to return from your ride.'

'Is Robert all right, Mama?' asked her daughter and as Lady Hadleigh gave a smile and a nod, Carolyn felt a weight slip from her shoulders.

She hurried to the library before going upstairs to her bedroom to change into a dress; she found her father with the letter in his hand.

'Such good news, my dear Carolyn, you must read it for yourself. It seems a long time since we had a letter from Robert, but this makes up for it.'

Carolyn sat in a low chair and picked up the letter. She read it carefully.

On board the Victory
                        Madeira, 14 May, 1805

My dear family
*This includes everyone. All these months,
we seem to have been chasing the French
around the Mediterranean and I have not
had an opportunity to write to you. You will
be surprised to hear that I am writing from
Madeira! We are on our way to the West
Indies, Lord Nelson having received
intelligence that Villeneuve has sailed
across the Atlantic with the combined
fleet—the Spanish fleet has joined with the
French. It was an agonizingly slow run out
of the Mediterranean due to the strong
westerly winds, but we are making up for it
by dipping south to Madeira to pick up the
steady trade winds to waft us across to the
West Indies. We have a very short stop here
so I must tell you my news as briefly as I
can. We are but ten of the line and pursuing
a fleet twice the size, but Lord Nelson
knows what he is about and we hope to
make swift progress. You will be pleased to
hear that I have all my certificates and
journals ready for the examination for
lieutenant; I expect to go to the Navy Office
next time I am home. I am twenty now and
have completed my six years so I am
entitled to be a lieutenant if I can pass the
examination. As it happens, due to an*

accident on board, I have been made acting-lieutenant and can walk the quarter deck. One of the lieutenants, Mr Maxwell Forbes by name, is from Maidstone and he is helping me with the navigation I need to know for the examination. We do not know what awaits us in the West Indies and I will try to send a letter to you from there. I am well.

Your loving son Robert

In the library, Carolyn looked at her father in delight. 'An acting-lieutenant! Oh, Papa, has he not done well? I am sure he will pass his examination especially if he has this Mr Forbes to help him. Fancy him being another naval man from Kent and so near to us.'

The whole family must have read the letter many times over before Carolyn was to meet Edwin again. It was the following morning and he took her in his gig towards Rye, skirting the Marsh, but going through the pretty villages of Ham Street and Warehorn. When they arrived at this last village, Carolyn knew why Edwin had brought her in this direction. Leaving the gig at the Woolpack Inn, they walked across the village green to the south of the village where Carolyn was puzzled to hear much shouting and laughter. She was soon to discover the reason, for they found the same activity as they had seen at Saltwood.

'They are digging the canal here, Edwin,'

she exclaimed.

He nodded. 'Yes, it is halfway along towards Rye. Pitt is losing no time.' He turned to her. 'I was interested in Robert's letter, Carolyn, for it confirms the news and rumours I have heard coming out of London.'

She was curious. 'Do you know why Villeneuve has gone to the West Indies?' she asked him.

'I think he is pretending to ravage the British ports and raid the sugar islands, but it is thought that he will give Nelson the slip and head back towards the English Channel. Some of the Spanish fleet seem to be lurking in the vicinity, and there is no doubt that Napoleon is planning an invasion. Pitt will do anything he can to defend the island.'

'It is a worrying time, Edwin.'

He looked at her. 'I could wish that you were safe in my arms at Ridley House,' he replied, and it was quietly said.

'Edwin!' Carolyn was both astonished and shocked at his words.

His arm crept round her waist and she could feel the pressure of his fingers through the soft sarsenet of her dress. It was such a hot day that she had dispensed with even a summer pelisse and was wearing a fine silk shawl over her shoulders.

'How much longer are you going to keep me waiting, Carolyn? You know now that Robert is safe and sound.'

'But there could be a naval battle when they reach the West Indies. You know my feelings on the matter very well. I refuse to marry until Robert is back in Ferrers Court again.' Carolyn knew that she must appear to be obstinate, but it was her dearest wish, and she would not be deflected from it by anyone.

'Shall I try and persuade you otherwise?'

'Whatever do you mean?' she asked him sharply.

They were now walking away from the busy scene at the canal and Edwin had paused in a copse of trees just outside Warehorn.

His hands slipped from her waist to her breasts which were barely covered by the wisp of a bodice of her dress. Carolyn gave a gasp and a shudder as he pulled the fabric down and bent his head to the soft skin.

She pulled herself from his arms, hastily covering herself up. She was furiously angry at the audacity of the behaviour of the gentleman she had said she would marry. She had felt no pleasure at the touch of his lips, only shock that the staid Edwin could behave in such a way.

'Edwin . . .' she blazed at him. 'How dare you? That is not the behaviour of a gentleman and it is certainly not the way to persuade me into an earlier marriage with you. What are you thinking of?'

'I want you for my wife, Carolyn. I need you. My future happiness depends upon it. I cannot bear to wait for you any longer.'

'Then you are going about it in a very strange way,' she snapped at him. 'You might have known that I was not the kind of young lady to be fondled and coaxed into a marriage I am not sure that I wish for in any case.'

'Whatever do you mean?' he asked her, and there was an edge to his voice. 'You must marry me; everything depends upon it.'

She was mystified at his words; it was not the first time he had said something of the sort. 'That is a strange remark to make, what do you mean by it?'

'It is you, Carolyn. I have tried to be patient and I do understand your wish to have Robert here at home, but you are tantalizing. Sometimes I feel I cannot wait.'

She was again astonished at his words. 'But, Edwin, it is only a matter of months. What has changed? You were always so proper and I admired you for it; perhaps that was a pretence to win me over.' Carolyn found herself with an inability to understand the change in Edwin Baillie. If she had loved him, she felt that she would have laughed at him and even delighted in his daring embraces. As it was, he seemed to be behaving out of character and it perplexed her.

He was speaking so strangely that she felt uneasy. If this had been the gentleman she loved and longed for, she could understand his feelings. But this was Edwin, the dull and proper Edwin, whose character had either undergone a change, or who was alluding to something she knew nothing about.

'I know that I have said it before, Edwin, but if you are so desperate for a wife, then I will let you go and you can find a nice, willing young lady in Ashford.'

'No, no, Carolyn,' he replied with unseemly haste. 'I must have you.'

The words sounded odd in Carolyn's ears, but she attributed them to the changed Edwin and she said nothing in reply, but took his arm and they walked back into the village.

For a few weeks, he returned to being his usual formal self and Carolyn had to wonder if she had imagined the incident near the canal at Warehorn.

It seemed to be no time at all before another letter came from Robert and during that time, there had come startling news of Villeneuve and the combined fleet.

Summer had slipped by into August and with it the summer weather had disappeared for the end of July was cold and dry with winds from the north.

Expecting Edwin and being dressed for riding—in a smart habit of dark red and not her usual, disgracefully shabby breeches and jacket—Carolyn entered the drawing-room to find Edwin and her father in an earnest and excited discussion over the news in *The Times*.

'Has there been some news?' she asked.

Edwin looked up and nodded, then returned to the newspaper. It was her father who enlightened her.

'Carolyn, it is not news of Lord Nelson, whom I suspect is still hunting for Villeneuve in the West Indies, but of Villeneuve himself. For Napoleon, it is a humiliation, but I do believe that we have been spared an imminent invasion.'

'Whatever do you mean? You are talking in riddles,' she replied, not understanding anything.

'You must read it for yourself, but I will tell you the most important part. It seems that Villeneuve was under orders from the Emperor to make haste from the West Indies—having drawn the British fleet over there and thus out of the way—and to join the rest of the Spanish fleet off Cape Ushant. Then between them, they could sail up the Channel and enable the French invasion of this country to take place.'

'You mean because there would be no British fleet to force them back?' she asked, wondering if she had got it right.

'Precisely so. But what did Villeneuve do? He disobeyed his orders and fought an indecisive battle out in the Atlantic off El Ferrol in Spain where Admiral Calder has a squadron.'

'Do you mean that the combined fleet was not destroyed?' Carolyn was beginning to understand.

'No, the weather was atrocious and Calder's squadron was outnumbered; they sailed back to El Ferrol. However, instead of proceeding to the Channel, Villeneuve turned south and the latest news is that he is harboured in Cadiz.'

Carolyn was thinking hard. 'If the combined fleet gave Lord Nelson the slip in the West Indies, we must hope that our ships will soon be sailing home.'

'Nonsense, Carolyn,' replied her father. 'Nelson will head back to the Mediterranean, you mark my words. He is not going to lose to France and Spain as easily as that.'

She nodded. 'Yes, we must remember the Battle of the Nile and hope for another victory as great as that.' She turned to her betrothed. 'Are we riding, Edwin? Or would you prefer to discuss the news with Papa?'

Edwin smiled at her. 'I am ready as soon as you are, my dear. Shall we ride up to the Downs or would you prefer the Marsh?'

He is trying to please me, thought Carolyn. What is in his mind now, I wonder? He always chooses the Downs and he also knows that I always ride over the Marsh when I want to be on my own.

'We will take the lane up towards Wye,' she replied. 'Then we can have a gallop on the Downs.'

'A good choice, Carolyn.' Edwin turned to

her father. 'I will leave you to the newspaper and the splendid news, Sir William.'

For many days, England was abuzz with the news of the withdrawal of the combined French and Spanish fleets into Cadiz harbour and wondered at Villeneuve's foolishness at disobeying Napoleon's orders. The threat of an imminent invasion was over and the population along the South Coast rested more happily in their beds. Lord Nelson was already a hero to them and they knew that he would protect the English Channel to the last.

A week later, Robert's letter from the West Indies arrived and the Ferrers Court family were able to read at first hand what they had already seen reported in *The Times*.

Sir William himself had ridden in to the Receiving Office in Ashford for the letter, glanced at its contents briefly, then carried it home so that he could read it to his family.

In the West Indies, 12 June 1805

Greetings to all of you from the West Indies. What a fruitless chase it has been, though we take pride in the fact that we covered the 3,000 miles from the Straits to Barbados in little more than three weeks, an average of 135 miles a day, it must be a record, I should think. I have just heard that the Curieux *sloop under Captain Bettesworth is being dispatched to England, so I must hurry. We reached Barbados on 4 June to receive a message from Brigadier-General Brereton at St Lucia that the combined fleet had been seen on 29 May steering towards Trinidad. Next morning, we were on our way there and Lord Nelson had made the signal 'Prepare For Battle'; every captain knew what was expected of him and his crew. There was no sight of the enemy at Tobago, and at Trinidad, they fired on us, mistaking us for Villeneuve. They had not seen him, so Brereton's intelligence had been false. We put out straight away and headed for Grenada, but when we reached Antigua earlier today, it was clear that the combined fleet had returned to Europe. Great frustration all round! We had been prepared for a fight, instead we return to Gibraltar tomorrow. I have had little time for study, but Maxwell is very encouraging about my chances. I expect to be in the Mediterranean again next time I write to you. I know that you have fears of Napoleon crossing the Channel, but rest assured that Lord Nelson will never let Villeneuve defeat him. He has our loyaly and he must have yours as well. I hope it will not be long before I am with you again.*

Your loving son Robert

Edwin seemed much cheered by this letter. He talked about it enthusiastically to Carolyn.

'Your father seems convinced that Lord Nelson will head for the Mediterranean again, but the good admiral does not know that Villeneuve has taken refuge at Cadiz and after the Atlantic voyage, the *Victory* and the other ships might need some attention at Portsmouth.' He and Carolyn were walking in the garden and he took her hand. 'Our time will soon be here, my dear Carolyn.'

Carolyn looked at him; she rarely thought of him as handsome, but when his face lost its usual solemnity, she liked what she saw. However, her feelings did not match her vision, for she felt dismayed rather than overjoyed at her imminent marriage. I expect every young lady feels the same, she thought, it is natural to have doubts. She promised herself to go and find out what Granny Harland had to say.

The opportunity came a few days later when Edwin was in London on a business matter. The days were warmer as they entered the month of August and Carolyn chose a longer route than usual to reach Newchurch. She rode by way of Ruckinge to see the progress of the Royal Military Canal and then had to go a long way round until she found a place where she could at last ford the rising waters.

'Miss Car'lyn,' Granny Harland greeted her cheerfully. 'And you not been to see me since you rode over to tell me you was engaged to that Mr Edwin Baillie. Here was I thinking that you must be Mrs Baillie by now and too grand to visit the likes of Granny Harland.'

Carolyn laughed as she sat down at the kitchen table. 'I have refused to marry Edwin until Robert is home, Granny. Once I am married, I will bring my children to visit you. Edwin does not like Romney Marsh as you know, but I will not let him stop me from bringing my children here.'

Granny Harland laughed. 'Miss Car'lyn, it is certain to be a long way round for you once this canal is finished. That's unless they put bridges across, of course. You'll never get over at Ruckinge.'

'Never mind, we can always drive by way of Ham Street instead; nothing will stop me coming, Granny Harland. That is, *if* I marry Edwin, of course.' Carolyn sounded defiant and Granny looked at her.

'What do you mean by that remark, young miss?' she asked quietly.

'It is why I have come. Edwin seems to think that Lord Nelson will bring the *Victory* into Portsmouth to be refitted or something; he thinks the ship will need it after chasing the French all the way across the Atlantic and back. Did you know about it, Granny?'

The old lady laughed. 'Because we live here in the middle of nowhere as you might put it, does not mean we're ignorant of what's going on in the world. Joel, he rides over to the inn at Ivychurch and they have a right gossip and soon put that there Napoleon to rights. There's not much we don't hear on. So it means you're expecting young Robert home soon, then, does it?'

Carolyn nodded. 'It will be wonderful to see him again and he will be able to take his examination to be a lieutenant. We are very proud of him.'

'What's the trouble then? You've come for old Granny's advice, I can see that.'

'I promised Edwin that I would marry him when Robert came home and I must keep my promise. But I don't feel sure about it, Granny. I can't understand myself sometimes. He has been so good to me and patient, too, and Papa and Mama think it is an excellent match for me. What is wrong with me, Granny?'

The reply came quickly. 'You've obeyed your head and not your heart. It was as I was telling you afore. There's nothing wrong in doing what your head says is proper, miss, many a good marriage is made that way. But now your heart isn't always in it, it's got left out, as it were. That's what's giving you the doubts, sure as eggs is eggs, as they say. You just stop worrying, Miss Car'lyn. If your ma and your pa thinks the gentleman is the right one for you, then you can be sure it'll turn out splendid, like. Only one thing I've got agin this gentleman as I've never met.'

'What is that?' Carolyn was curious.

'He's not keen on the Marsh, or so you say.'

Carolyn laughed then and felt a measure of relief. 'He is a city gentleman, Granny, and not used to our wild ways! He likes the Downs and often takes me towards Maidstone and I like it there, too. The Marsh is my own; it is in my blood and nothing can take it away from me. I shall still find the time to ride over to see you; nothing will keep me away.'

'Then I'm glad to hear it,' said Granny. 'You'll be all right, Miss Car'lyn, as long as you can get on your favourite horse and come out and see the dykes and the ditches and feel the salt on your face. You won't go far wrong. Forget your worries if you're sure he's the right gentleman. All young misses get nervous afore their wedding day. Now I'm going to get you a tankard of small ale as I reckon you needs it. Put some heart into you, it will.'

Carolyn smiled and said thank you; she enjoyed her drink and rode away reassured. She stopped for a long time before she reached the boundaries of Ferrers Court, looking back across the flat expanse of Romney Marsh as though she was looking into eternity.

FOUR

Edwin had been quite correct in his assumption that the *Victory* would need a refit and that Robert would soon be home again. On 18 August, Lord Nelson anchored off Portsmouth; it was reported that he was depressed and anxious about his reception, but without knowing it, the tired admiral had become a legend and was greeted by cheering crowds all the way to London.

At Ferrers Court, Carolyn and Lizzie were sitting at their embroidery in the drawing-room when they heard a commotion outside the front door; the sound of wheels on the gravel, of running footsteps from the stables, shouts and laughter.

They rushed to the window in time to see two naval gentlemen jumping down from a gig.

The two sisters shouted in one voice. 'It's Robert . . . it's Robert . . .'

Carolyn was at the door before she had time to hear Lizzie say, 'But who is it with him?'

In the pandemonium which followed, Robert was hugging them all in turn, for Lady Hadleigh had appeared in the drawing-room and Miss Grimble had brought Ben and Lucy down from the schoolroom. Amongst tears, squeals, shouts and laughter, he tried to introduce his companion.

Carolyn, amidst all the confusion, had been conscious of the searching glance from the tall naval officer who had followed Robert into the room. He was standing quietly to one side while the family greeted Robert in noisy excitement. The visitor had noticed very quickly that Carolyn's tall darkness set her aside and he was interested; he had easily guessed that this was the sister of whom Robert had told him so much.

The introductions came at last.

'Mama, Carolyn, Lizzie . . . this is my friend and mentor Lieutenant Maxwell Forbes. He is from Maidstone, but his family spend the summer months in Scotland, so I hope that you don't mind, Mama, I have invited Maxwell to spend our leave here with us at Ferrers Court.' Robert turned to his friend. 'Maxwell, may I introduce you to my mama, Lady Hadleigh. Where is Papa?' he asked his mother.

Lieutenant Forbes was not only very tall and dark, he bore classic good looks and keen grey eyes—he, like Robert, was very tanned. He made his bow to Lady Hadleigh and received a smile and an encouraging nod in return.

'We are delighted to welcome you to stay with us, Lieutenant,' she said warmly. 'I know that my husband will say the same, for we have heard nothing but praise of you in Robert's letters. Sir William will want to thank you. He is somewhere about the estate at the moment;

I believe him to be visiting one of the farms with his steward.'

Carolyn was standing quietly by, but there came a sudden realization that her heart had quickened and that she was holding her hands together in a tight clasp.

Robert put an arm round her shoulders and drew her forward. 'Maxwell, this is my dear Carolyn. I hope that you and she will deal well together for she is very precious to me. Carolyn, I am pleased to introduce you to Maxwell who has become such a good friend.'

Carolyn found both her hands taken as the lieutenant made his bow. Their eyes met and she found herself unable to describe her emotions; admiration, yes, but there was a trust, a hope, a current of feeling which at the same time thrilled and dismayed her. She had remembered Edwin.

'I am very pleased to meet you, Lieutenant Forbes.' She gave the newcomer her greeting pleasantly enough, then turned to Robert. 'I have become engaged to Edwin Baillie while you have been away, Rob, and I have promised to marry him as soon as you returned. Do you remember him?'

'The lawyer from Ashford? Respectable enough, but rather a dull stick, I thought.'

Lizzie had joined them, full of excitement. 'That is just what I said, Robert, but he and Carolyn have become very firm friends and he is always very civil to me. At least he does not treat me as a child.'

Robert hugged her and laughed. 'You are certainly no child, Lizzie, you have become a very pretty young lady.'

'Thank you, Robert,' Lizzie replied, and turned to speak to the lieutenant as she could see that Carolyn was wanting to be with Robert.

Wine was brought into the drawing-room, together with small cakes and macaroons. It was in the middle of this celebration that Edwin arrived.

Carolyn went into the entrance hall to greet him when she heard him announced.

'Edwin, you will never believe it. Robert is home and he has brought his lieutenant friend with him; Maxwell Forbes. I remember telling you that he was helping Robert with his navigation studies. Do come in and I will introduce you.'

But Edwin was gripping her arm and seemed to be in some agitation. 'Robert home? Thank God. Do you know how long he will be here, Carolyn? We can be married at last.'

Carolyn thought she had misheard him. 'Married, Edwin? But they are only here for a few weeks, until the beginning of September, I think. How can we possibly arrange it?'

He was frowning at her. 'Carolyn, you have always promised to marry me as soon as Robert returned and now is the time. We can have the banns called at our church in Ashford and we will be married before Robert has to return to his duty.' His frown was replaced by a keen enthusiasm; Carolyn afterwards thought that it was an expression of relief. He gripped her hands. 'I am so pleased, my dear, let us go and tell your mama.'

Carolyn was stammering. 'I know that I promised you, Edwin . . . but the time is so short . . . how would Mama arrange everything and a wedding gown to be made, as well? It is not possible, you must realize it.'

She had never before seen the hard expression which came into Edwin's eyes. 'It *is* possible, Carolyn, and I insist on keeping you to your promise. You know very well that I have longed for the day when you would become my wife and we can settle at Ridley House.'

Carolyn felt bewildered. This was a strange Edwin, but he was so pleased and eager and he was right in saying that she had promised him.

He leaned forward and kissed her gently on the lips, his hand on her shoulder. 'It has all come right, I am very, very pleased. Come, let us go into the drawing-room.'

As Carolyn entered the room at Edwin's side, she again felt the eyes of Maxwell Forbes upon her, but she ignored him and went straight up to her mother, leaving Robert to introduce his friend to Edwin.

'Mama, I wish to talk to you. It is urgent.

You know that I promised to marry Edwin as soon as Robert returned; I told you so when you questioned the delay in our nuptials. Edwin says that the wedding can take place now. He says that there is enough time to call the banns before Robert goes back to Portsmouth. But my wedding gown and all the arrangements, and a dress for Lizzie for I have promised that she should be a bridesmaid . . . Why, what is it, Mama?'

She broke off and asked her question as she saw tears streaming down her mother's face.

'My dear girl, it is too much joy all in the space of an hour. Robert here and you to marry Edwin. Of course it can be done. We have the satin for your gown and good Miss Hargreaves in Ashford will have it made up in a few days and a pretty gown for Lizzie, too. And we will have a wedding breakfast here at Ferrers Court and it will be such a happy occasion with Robert being here and his friend with him. Is he not a handsome gentleman, the lieutenant? Do you think he would do for Lizzie?'

If Carolyn had not felt so disturbed, she would have laughed merrily at this remark. 'Oh, Mama, Lizzie is only just out of the schoolroom though I admit to her being very pretty. The lieutenant must be thirty years of age at least, I should say.'

Lady Hadleigh sighed. 'Yes, you are quite right; it was just a happy thought. Now we

57

must lose no time in making our arrangements. It is sure to be a lovely occasion and Robert here, too, it is almost too much good news in one day after all the worry we have had with the threat of invasion and Robert being at sea . . . Oh, there you are, Robert. Have you heard Carolyn's good news?'

Robert nodded. 'Yes, Edwin has just told me. He seems to want to rush you to the altar before we return to Portsmouth. Are you happy, Carolyn, are you sure it is what you want?'

Carolyn made herself face up to her feelings. My head rules, she was telling herself. Edwin is a good person, I should never do better and I cannot go back on my word.

So she spoke with enthusiasm. 'Robert, everything is happening at once! You safely home and bringing your friend with you and both of you looking so bronzed after your summer in the Mediterranean and crossing to the Indies. And now the wedding to think about. Mama is pleased and it is all very exciting. I do not know what Papa will say when he comes in; it has all happened so suddenly.'

Robert put his arms around her. 'I am very pleased for you if it is what you want. I am sure that Edwin will make you a good husband and he is not taking you far from Ferrers Court which is very nice for Mama.' He gave a laugh then and his fingers tightened on her shoulders. 'I had hoped to marry you off to Maxwell, but it seems that it is not to be.'

'Robert,' Carolyn replied with a laugh, 'you are as outrageous as ever. Do you take your lieutenant's examination while you are here?'

'Yes, I do; I will be glad to have it over and done with and must hope that I pass. I think I told you that I have been acting-lieutenant for a while so perhaps that will give me a better chance. Maxwell and I are going to London next week, but I promise to be back in time to see you married.'

Carolyn gave him a kiss on the cheek. 'We all hope that you will pass. We are very proud of you, Robert.'

They all sat down to a gay luncheon and Edwin returned to Ashford during the afternoon, having waited until Sir William returned to make sure that the plans met with his approval.

'Splendid, dear boy, splendid,' was Sir William's reply, when Edwin told him of the plan; he was in high good spirits with the return of his son. 'It could not be better. I will be glad to see you settled with Carolyn at Ridley House though no doubt you will be tripping off on some honeymoon or other.'

Edwin and Carolyn had been discussing this and he had his reply ready. 'Ridley House is to be refurbished, so I have acquired a carriage and a good coachman and we plan to journey down into Cornwall. I believe that the coastline there is very beautiful and Carolyn favours the sea.'

'A very good idea and thoughtful of you, I must say. Though it will be a hard day for us, sending you and Carolyn off and Robert back to Portsmouth at the same time. But Lady Hadleigh and I are very proud of our family and it pleases us to know that Carolyn is being placed in such good hands.'

Edwin departed and Robert closeted himself with his father in the library; for a few minutes, the drawing-room was quiet and Carolyn found herself on her own with Lieutenant Maxwell Forbes.

All the morning, she had been aware of his presence, for she had often felt his eyes on her. Now that she was with him on her own for the first time, she felt unaccountably shy and tried to steer the conversation into safe waters.

'Lieutenant Forbes, we have to thank you for helping Robert with his studies,' she said quietly, for some reason not daring to look at him.

'He is an apt pupil and I am assured of his success.' He stood up suddenly. 'But, dammit, Carolyn, I cannot say what I have to say in a drawing-room—can we walk in the garden? And my name is Maxwell, if you please.'

Carolyn stood up with a sense of shock at his words and hoped that Robert was not in any kind of trouble.

60

'Yes, by all means,' she said. 'The shrubbery at the side of the house is very secluded. I will fetch a pelisse.'

'No, come as you are; it is not cold and you look beautiful.' She looked up at him at last and could not read his expression. 'You are talking nonsense, sir.'

He laughed and took her arm. 'Not a bit of it; I know beauty when I see it. Come.'

'I will just go and tell Mama,' she said hastily.

'Certainly, I will be at the front door.'

Sir William Hadleigh was proud of his shrubbery and had reason to be so; there were shrubs for all seasons and for the winter he had taken care to plant evergreen shrubs for their interesting foliage. It now being August, the rhododendrons were still in bloom and a hibiscus flowered freely in a secluded corner.

Carolyn walked slowly at the lieutenant's side; they were both of them dark-haired, they were both tall, but she felt as though he towered above her, his personality was so dominant.

They reached a corner of the shrubbery where Sir William had placed several wooden seats, but the lieutenant did not sit down or invite Carolyn to do so.

His hand still on her arm, Maxwell Forbes had turned Carolyn to face him. He had talked quietly about their experiences in the West Indies as they had walked from the house and although his voice had been subdued, Carolyn could sense an undercurrent of feeling between them. It disturbed her and she could not understand it, except for an odd notion that they could quarrel quite easily.

Now she was forced to look up at him.

'Tell me, Miss Carolyn Hadleigh, what is all this nonsense about you being married to Mr Edwin Baillie before Robert and I return to sea?' His voice was cool and hit her as with a slender knife entering her heart.

'Whatever do you mean, sir?'

'You know quite well that you cannot marry him.'

Carolyn felt anger then. What was this handsome stranger about? 'Of course I am going to marry him, I have known it for nearly a year. The wedding only awaited Rob's safe return.'

Suddenly his fingers slipped from her arm and she felt his hands in a firm grasp about her waist. In her surprise, she did not struggle.

'You cannot marry him, my dear Carolyn, because you are going to marry me.'

Her head shot up; her eyes met a glance from grey eyes which were at the same time passionate and determined.

'You like to talk nonsense, Lieutenant,' she found herself saying coolly, even though her heart pounded. 'You have known me for only two minutes and I am engaged to marry another gentleman; I would be glad if you would take your hands from my waist.'

'It disturbs you? I am pleased of that for it is what I want to do. As soon as I saw you across the room, I knew I would marry you; that you were the young lady I had waited ten long years to meet. You knew it, too; I saw it in your eyes.'

'Balderdash,' Carolyn exclaimed, but felt unsure of herself. His hands still held her waist and she was aware of liking the feeling it gave her. But her words belied her feelings. 'I say it again, sir, you are talking nonsense. I am quite determined on marrying Edwin for I know that he will be a good husband to me. I made him a promise and now that Robert is home, I will not break it. Edwin has gone to see the rector at this very moment to arrange to have the banns called. I will be his wife in three weeks' time.'

'Not if I have my way in this,' came the astonishing reply.

'You are making me dislike you more and more every minute, Lieutenant. I believe you must be nothing more than an audacious rascal. You do not know me, you know nothing of me and here you are trying to dissuade me from marrying the gentleman of my choice.'

'I do know you, Carolyn. I have not been months at sea with Robert to learn nothing about you. I know how you love to ride across Romney Marsh with nothing but the horizon of the sea in the distance; I longed to be with you in that wild and desolate place. To feel the wind and the salt spray in the air, to see the distant line of the greyness of the Channel. You were with me in my dreams of Romney Marsh and now you are here in my arms.'

Carolyn was transfixed by his words; was this the gentleman of her dreams? The gentleman to stir her heart and not her head? She was silent.

'You have no words, Carolyn?'

She looked at him dumbly and then felt his fingers creep from her waist to take the weight of her full rounded breasts which strained against the thin muslin of her dress.

The sensation in her body alarmed her and she tore herself from his grasp to jump back and face him angrily.

'How dare you. I never thought to say the words but you are nothing more than a lecherous beast. You might be a good friend to Robert, but I want nothing more to do with you . . .' She spat out the words and started to run towards the house.

'No, Carolyn, you do not understand . . . I love you . . .'

These last words echoed in her head as she rushed upstairs and flung herself on her bed. Her body ached, her heart ached and then she sobbed.

I could have loved him, she found herself thinking, but he is no gentleman. I could wish that Robert had not brought him here and now, how am I going to face seeing him again? I heard those last words. He said he loved me, but I think he lusted after me, that is all it was. He has not been in female company for a very long time, after all. I am safe with dear Edwin, even if he does not excite the senses, and he will make me a good husband. I have said so before and it is what I must always remember.

For two days, she avoided Lieutenant Maxwell Forbes. It was not difficult as he and Robert rode out, round the estate and over the Marsh. They met only at dinnertime when her father and Robert dominated the conversation and she did not raise her eyes to meet the demanding ones of the lieutenant. After dinner, Robert and Maxwell joined Sir William in the library for their port, and in the drawing-room, Lady Hadleigh talked endlessly of her plans for the wedding. Carolyn hardly listened; she heard the lieutenant's voice rather than that of her mama and the same words repeated in her mind again and again: I love you.

For two days, Edwin did not appear and Carolyn was puzzled. She had expected him to come and tell her that he had arranged for the banns to be called on the coming Sunday.

On the third day, Robert and Maxwell did not ride out as they were preparing for their trip to London so that Robert could take his examination at the Navy Office.

Sir William owned a small town house in

North Audley Street and he had sent word to his housekeeper to have the house ready for the visit of the two gentlemen.

Edwin still had not appeared and Carolyn found herself sitting on the sofa with Maxwell in the drawing-room. Her mother and Lizzie were somewhere in the house discussing wedding preparations and Robert was not to be seen. It was the first time she had been on her own with Maxwell since the confrontation in the shrubbery.

'Carolyn,' he was saying, rather formally, 'I shall not see you for a week or two and I have it on my conscience that I behaved improperly towards you when we were walking in the shrubbery. I do not wish to withdraw my words, for it is true that I have come to love you—indeed, I think I loved you even before I saw you—but I realize that my sentiments are not returned and that you are set on a marriage to Edwin. You must have your own reason for wanting to marry him, but I happen to think that you are making a mistake. By the time we return from London, it will be the day of your wedding and I must wish you joy. Will you forgive my impetuous behaviour?'

Carolyn had not expected this and she felt almost choked with her own feelings. She had been very rude to him and did not deserve such a fulsome apology.

She turned to him with a shy smile. 'Maxwell, I do not wish to part on bad terms.

66

You have been such a good friend to Robert and I will never forget that. Thank you. I hope that you will enjoy your visit to London.'

He smiled gratefully. 'Shall we kiss and be friends?'

'No, Maxwell . . .' she started to say, but he had put his arms around her and kissed her quickly on the lips; then before she could move away, his lips strayed to her soft, bare shoulder.

Carolyn gave a shiver of delight and as she did so, the door of the drawing-room was opened and her mother and Lizzie stood there followed by an astonished Edwin.

He did not stand still for long; he quickly took in the scene, bounded over to the sofa where Carolyn and Maxwell had sprung apart and hit out at Maxwell, his fist crashing into the lieutenant's temple.

'How dare you embrace Carolyn. How dare you! She is to be my wife. Stand up, damn you, and take what is coming to you, or I will call you out for your deuced impertinence.'

Maxwell had hardly felt the force of Edwin's blow and he got up, took hold of the young gentleman's coat and gave him a strong blow to the middle of his body. Maxwell was a tall and strong man, Edwin was neither. He fell to the floor and lay there amid screams from the ladies and angry words from Maxwell.

'That is what I have to say to you, Mr Edwin Baillie, you can lie there as long as you like. I shall not see you again for I will be in London by this time tomorrow. But if you can hear me, know that you are going to marry the young lady I love and would care for with my life if I had the chance.'

Edwin had not moved. Without another glance at Carolyn, Lieutenant Maxwell Forbes stormed out of the room.

FIVE

There was a silence in the drawing-room at Ferrers Court as the door closed on Lieutenant Maxwell Forbes. Lady Hadleigh, Lizzie and Carolyn were all perfectly still, shocked by what had occurred. Then there came a groan from the prostrate figure on the floor and Carolyn found herself kneeling at the side of her betrothed.

Slowly Edwin sat up, his hand to his chest. 'Winded by the bastard . . .' he managed to say. 'Where is he?'

'Hush, Edwin,' said Carolyn. 'See if you can stand up and I will help you to a chair.' She turned to look at Lady Hadleigh. 'Mama, please will you fetch some brandy or ring for it or something. I do not think Edwin is hurt, just winded. It was quite a blow.'

Lady Hadleigh looked dazed with events

and Lizzie jumped up eagerly.

'I will fetch the brandy; I know where it is, Papa keeps it in the library.' Then she added, 'Perhaps we should all have some, because of the shock, that is. Maxwell should not have hit poor Edwin like that . . . oh dear, I will go quickly.'

Carolyn had helped Edwin sit down and when Lizzie returned carefully carrying a tray with the brandy and some glasses, he seemed glad to drink it.

'Bastard,' he said almost incoherently. 'Shouldn't have called him that, but then, he should not have been kissing you, Carolyn. What is it all about?'

Carolyn herself had taken a sip of the brandy and felt better for it. 'Edwin,' she said. 'I can explain everything, but I would rather that we were on our own. Take some brandy and we will go and sit on the seat near the front door. Maxwell has gone. He and Robert are preparing to go to London at first light tomorrow. I shall most probably never see him again.'

These last words, while seeming to Carolyn as though they were going to break her heart, appeared to reassure Edwin.

He stood up and looked at Lady Hadleigh. 'I apologize, ma'am, for such a scene in your drawing-room. It was more than a fellow could stand to see his would-be bride being kissed by another gentleman. I thought with my fists instead of asking for an explanation; then the bastard . . . I apologize for my language, ma'am . . . knocked me out.' He turned to Carolyn. 'Yes, we must talk the matter over quietly between us, I think that I can walk as far as the garden.'

On the seat under the trees to the side of the front door of Ferrers Court, Edwin still looked shaky and Carolyn could not help but feel guilty at the whole episode.

'Now, young lady,' Edwin said pettishly. 'What have you to say about the disgraceful scene I walked in upon? Seeing you being kissed by another gentleman was more than flesh and blood could stand. I am not sorry that I hit the fellow, but I still want an explanation.'

Carolyn felt miserable. Have I really said that I will marry him, she asked herself? Is it too late to cry off? I know now that I do not love him as I should, but then I believe I knew that all along. I still went ahead thinking that it was the right step to take in my life.

'Edwin, I am sorry that you found Maxwell kissing me; I can explain it, but if you would prefer me to cry off, then I will do so.'

He looked alarmed and sounded it, too. 'Cry off now? My dear girl, the banns are being called tomorrow and the wedding only weeks away. No, no, you cannot cry off. I will not have it, for it would ruin everything. I did not consider Lieutenant Forbes to be a

70

scoundrel, but if he was forcing his attentions on you, then I am glad that I hit him.'

Some of Edwin's words puzzled Carolyn, but she wanted to put things right between them. She would have to tell some half-truths.

'Maxwell and I had a quarrel the other day—never mind what it was about, it was quite trivial—but I walked away from him. Just now, when you came into the drawing-room, he had apologized and told me that he and Robert were going to London first thing in the morning. He asked me if he could kiss me goodbye and before I had time to make any protest, he had kissed me and you walked in . . .'

'But he had his arms around you.'

'Did he? I did not notice, I was too put out by him saying that he wanted to kiss me goodbye.' Carolyn was speaking quietly, her feelings were muddled and she did not know how Edwin was going to respond.

He surprised her. 'And that is all? A storm in a tea cup and all down to my jealousy. I do love you very much, Carolyn, and our wedding day will soon be here now. Then we will have our few weeks in Cornwall together while Ridley House is being made ready for you; I have been living in just two of the rooms all this time, and I do want it to be nice for you to return to. This is going to be a happy time for us and once we are married, all my worries will be over.'

If Carolyn was somewhat perplexed by his sentiments, she said nothing. It had been wrong of Maxwell to kiss her, it had been wrong of her to enjoy the kiss; but she must put all dangerous thoughts of Maxwell Forbes from her mind and concentrate on the kindness and thoughtfulness of Edwin Baillie.

*   *   *

Ferrers Court seemed quiet after Robert and Maxwell had left for London and to Carolyn's surprise, Edwin did not appear for several days. When he did come, he seemed subdued and he did not stay long.

He was both kind and polite, but Carolyn could not help but feel that he was rather distant; it was as though he had something on his mind apart from his approaching marriage.

She soon forgot Edwin's lack of attention in the whirl of preparations for the wedding which was fixed for the second week in September.

There were many visits to the dressmaker in Ashford and both Carolyn and Lizzie were pleased with the end results. Carolyn's wedding gown was of a rich cream satin with a flounce of matching lace; Lady Hadleigh said that she looked beautiful in it and they laid it carefully on the bed in one of the spare bedrooms, covering it with butter muslin from one of the farms.

Lizzie was as excitable as ever and walked up and down the drawing-room very slowly in her pretty dress of blue jaconet muslin with an embroidered bodice; she said that it was to show that she could be dignified if she chose to be.

Carolyn did not have time to have any doubts. Robert and Maxwell were still in London, but expected to be back again in time for the wedding.

A brief note came from Robert which pleased them very much; it arrived a few days before the wedding.

Dear Family
I know that you will be pleased to hear that I have passed my examnation for the lieutenancy. I expect to be full lieutenant when I take my place on the Victory *again. Maxwell and I are just off to White's to celebrate and perhaps to risk a few guineas at the faro tables. We hope to be with you very soon.*
Your loving son Robert

With the wedding day only two days away and Robert and Maxwell not returned, Carolyn began to feel nervous and had a slight tiff with Edwin. It was after morning service at the church in Ashford and took place in the churchyard as they were walking towards the waiting carriages. For more than a year, it had been Edwin's custom to return with the family to Ferrers Court for his Sunday dinner.

That morning, he was apologetic and in Carolyn's eyes, seemed slightly fidgety; she guessed that he was feeling as nervous as she did herself and tried to be understanding.

'Carolyn,' he said to her. 'I will not return to Ferrers Court with you today, if you will excuse me. I take delivery of my carriage tomorrow and I want to make sure that everything is in order with the coachman whom I have engaged.'

Carolyn frowned. 'But, Edwin, you could do all that and then come to us for your dinner later on. I feel in need of your support. It is only two days now, you know.'

'Yes, I do know that, my dear, and the next time I see you will be in the church. I know that you will be looking very beautiful and that it will be a most successful and enjoyable occasion for us all.' He was speaking rather nervously and as Carolyn looked at him and caught a glimpse of uncertainty in his eyes, she felt her spirits flag. His words had seemed unnaturally forced and she wondered if he was regretting his decision to marry her.

'Do you want to marry me, Edwin?' she asked, and her voice held a nervous harshness.

'Want to marry you? Of course I do. What a silly question. I've got to marry you.'

Carolyn was mystified by this last statement and rebellion flared up in her. 'Whatever do

74

you mean by that remark? You have not *got* to marry me if you would rather not. There is still time for me to cry off.' She was alarmed to hear her voice becoming shrill.

But her tone had the effect of calming Edwin. 'Cry off, Carolyn, what are you saying? Of course, I do not want you to cry off. The days before you become my wife are going too slowly for me. But I do not care for all the fuss, I am a quiet gentleman, as you know. It is understandable for Sir William Hadleigh of Ferrers Court to want a grand affair for the wedding of his daughter and while it makes me very happy, it also makes me very nervous. Tell me that you are a little nervous, too, my dear Carolyn.'

She smiled then, for he had sounded like the sensible Edwin whom she respected so much. 'Yes, Edwin, I do feel nervous and I can understand you not wanting to come to Sunday dinner with us.' Her voice dropped to a whisper. 'The next time I see you it will be in the church, just as you said.'

He took her hand in his and she felt a strength she had not expected. 'My sweet girl, I cannot wait. Off you go now and give my apologies to your parents, I am sure that they will understand. They are waiting in the carriage for you.'

She expressed her gratitude by pressing his hand, said no more and hurried to join her family.

Two days later and the night before the wedding, all was excitement at Ferrers Court as Robert and Maxwell returned. They all celebrated Robert's success with champagne and after dinner, Maxwell, who had said little to her and seemed quiet beside his ebullient friend, asked Carolyn to take a walk around the garden with him.

Carolyn hesitated; it had momentarily stirred her feelings as she had greeted him on his arrival, but such was her state of nervous excitement that she immediately put all thoughts of the handsome lieutenant on one side and worried more about whether she would trip over her gown as she walked up the aisle in the church the following morning.

She had thought that Maxwell had joined her papa and Robert in the library when dinner was over, but as she returned to the drawing-room, she found him at her side.

'Carolyn, I will see little of you tomorrow with such a houseful and the next day, Robert and I will be on our way back to Portsmouth. Please walk in the garden with me for a few minutes so that we can say goodbye.'

'It will soon be dark, Maxwell,' she replied. She wanted to be with him one last time, but she was afraid of her feelings; not only that, she was afraid of *his* feelings as she remembered the kiss which had caused the uproar the last time they had been together.

'It is sunset,' he declared. 'It will be very

76

pleasant out-of-doors, but you will need your pelisse.'

'Yes, Maxwell,' she found herself saying, and her feet seemed to take her upstairs to her bedroom of their own volition.

Outside the house, it seemed natural that they should walk towards the shrubbery, but they did not sit down. It had been a fine September day and calm; the sun was now low in the west and the sky had taken its golden glow. The shadows were long and the air was quiet.

Carolyn, tense with the anticipation of the events of the next day, found herself listening to the calming voice of Maxwell Forbes and forgetting her fears.

'Carolyn, I have brought you here to say goodbye to you and that, to me at least, is a sad thought. But now we are here in this lovely half-light, it will seem easier to say all that I want to say. I have thought about you many times while Robert and I have been in London.'

She gave a low chuckle. 'I think, if you were to be honest, Maxwell, that you would have been thinking more of what you were winning or losing at the gaming tables.'

'Minx,' he said with a smile. 'Come and sit down with me and give me your hands so that I can talk seriously to you . . . just as though I was your uncle.'

Carolyn laughed then and the laughter

seemed to release the tension of her feelings. 'Maxwell Forbes, anyone less like an uncle than you, it would be hard to imagine!'

'I am determined to say the words which I know your father should be saying to you, but I know that he will not because he is so keen on this match for his daughter. Edwin seems to be a gentleman of substance and that pleases Sir William, does it not?'

'Yes, he *is* pleased; he likes Edwin.'

'But do *you* like Edwin, Carolyn?' The question dropped into the silence of the still September evening.

Carolyn was startled and looked across at him as they sat side by side on the wooden seat. His expression was serious; there was no hint of any emotion in his eyes which were grey and steady.

'What a strange thing to ask, Maxwell. Of course I like Edwin; surely you must know that I would not have agreed to marry him if I had not liked him sufficiently.' She stopped speaking; she had suddenly remembered their last encounter in this very place. 'I want no repeat of our last meeting here; you behaved disgracefully, if I remember correctly.'

'You were very tempting to me. I longed for you to be mine, but if you are certain that you are doing the right thing in marrying the sober Edwin, then I must respect your wishes. Don't be frightened of me, Carolyn, I have myself well in hand.'

'No, of course, I am not frightened of you; you are a good friend to Robert and I know Robert well enough to understand that he admires and respects you. I will do the same.'

'You are determined on this marriage?'

Carolyn looked deep into her heart and refused to obey her feelings. She spoke slowly and carefully. 'I do not pretend to love Edwin with a great passion; that is not for everyone. But I like everything about him. He is not only a respected lawyer in the town, but his disposition is always one of kindness and consideration. He loves me and I enter into the marriage state with every confidence.'

'But not happiness?' he asked quietly.

'Happiness?'

'Yes, are you happy?'

Carolyn nodded. 'Yes, I suppose I am.' She paused for a moment. 'Maxwell, I have thought about it so much. I will be honest with you. Somehow you are the kind of person with whom one can be entirely honest.'

'I am glad of that,' he murmured.

'I suppose every girl dreams about love, and we read about love, too, not only in the novels of Mrs Radcliffe, but in Shakespeare, as well. But romantic love in that sense is a rare thing and I happen to think that a good marriage can be based on a mutual liking, respect and understanding. All those things I have with Edwin and that is why I am going to marry him . . .' She broke off. 'Goodness gracious, it is tomorrow morning. Whatever am I doing sitting here talking to you? We have family arriving this evening, too; my aunt and uncle and two cousins. I must be there to greet them or it will seem so rude. I will see you tomorrow, Maxwell.'

'In the distance,' he told her and gave a rueful laugh. 'Then Robert and I go off in the afternoon; that is why I wanted these few minutes with you. I wanted to be sure that you are doing the right thing.'

She looked at him, feeling puzzled. 'Does it matter to you?' she asked.

'More than you will ever know . . .' He broke off. 'Now we *will* say farewell. May I kiss you on the cheek? No more, I promise you.'

She turned her cheek to him and he touched it gently with his lips 'Goodbye, my dearest Carolyn, and I wish you every happiness,' he said, and he stood up beside her.

Carolyn rose and looked at him; their eyes met and there was naked feeling in their expressions. She did not know how it happened, but suddenly she was in his arms and he was kissing her fiercely. She found herself wanting the kiss, returning it; she felt the wonderful strength of the whole of his body against hers.

It was Maxwell who pushed her away and she stood there looking dazed.

'Go back to the house, Carolyn, they will be

wondering where you are. You have told me what I wanted to know. Whatever happens in my life, I will never forget you. Go now, please go.'

With a sob, Carolyn turned and ran back through the shrubbery. I love Maxwell and I am going to marry Edwin. Whatever have I done, she asked herself? But as she neared the house and saw her uncle's carriage, she knew that love had come too late. She would forget Maxwell Forbes in her happy life with Edwin and their children; she could remember Maxwell, she could dream of him, she could not love him.

By the time she had greeted her noisy relatives, she was calm again; they were happy to be there and she was happy to have them with her. She went to bed, but slept little; when she did awake, it was her wedding morning.

Afterwards, Carolyn could remember very little from the time of her waking to the time of being helped into the carriage by her father. She and Lizzie and their parents travelled in one carriage, and were followed by Miss Grimble and Ben and Lucy in a smaller carriage. Both children had been given new outfits and they were excited, yet well behaved.

The last carriage contained Uncle George Hadleigh with Aunt Prim, as they called her, with their two daughters, Jane and Mary; the two girls were near to Lizzie in age and the cousins knew each other well.

Robert was to be Edwin's groomsman and had gone ahead with Maxwell. To her dismay, Carolyn had discovered that none of Edwin's family would be present at the wedding; neither of his parents was still alive and his only brother, James, lived in Northumberland. There was a longstanding quarrel between the two brothers over James's inheritance from his father; he was the eldest and had inherited everything including the family mansion near Alnwick. Edwin had received next to nothing and James was not a generous man.

Carolyn felt amazingly calm. She knew that her gown was beautiful and that it suited her, her mama and Lizzie had told her so many times. She had also had new dresses and a warmer pelisse made and these were all ready and packed for the journey into Cornwall.

She did not have time to think of Maxwell; last night being already part of the past. She thought little about Edwin either, but did wonder if she would be shy with him once they were on their own as man and wife.

They arrived at the church in Ashford on the stroke of eleven o' clock and it immediately became apparent that something unusual had occurred. The first thing that Carolyn noticed was that both Robert and Maxwell were standing in the church porch. They should have been inside the church and both of them were looking anxious.

Robert walked over to the family coach and

opened the door. 'Carolyn, Papa, Edwin has not yet arrived and we cannot understand why he is late for his own wedding; he is so punctilious in all things that we are afraid that something must be amiss. You had better all come and take your places while Maxwell and I decide what to do for the best. We felt that we could not go in search of Edwin until you had arrived.'

Carolyn listened as in a trance. Edwin not here? Edwin who was so meticulous about time and place, who had never been known to be a minute late for any meeting or function? Robert helped her down from the carriage and then Lizzie carefully arranged her sister's gown.

Trying not to worry, she held her father's arm and walked into the church; Maxwell accompanied Lady Hadleigh with Lizzie at their side.

The church was full and the hum of chatter was silenced as the bride appeared; all the tenants of the Ferrers Court farms had been invited and there were many friends and neighbours from round about Aldington and from Ashford itself.

But it was noticeable that the pews on the groom's side were empty; Edwin had not even invited his attorney partners from Cullen, Clarke and Cullen, or any of his household. Carolyn found it disquieting.

Knowing that something was very wrong,

she did not fail to notice the hush as she sat down and concentrated on all the beautiful September flowers which decorated the altar and the window sills.

She sat with her mother and father and Lizzie in the front pew, conscious of the empty pew on the other side of the aisle which should have been occupied by Edwin, Robert and Maxwell.

The sound of the organ she found comforting as it seemed to cover the awkward silence all around her. Edwin must be ill, she was saying to herself, then whispered the words to her father who gave a nod. He took her hand and held it tight.

At last she heard footsteps down the aisle, but she did not turn her head.

It was Robert.

'Robert,' whispered Carolyn, 'do you think Edwin is ill?'

'Try not to worry, Carolyn,' replied her brother firmly. 'Maxwell has taken the gig to Ridley House to find out what has happened; he will soon be here. Sit back and listen to the music; I will stay with you.' He leaned across them. 'Try not to cry, Mama, all will be well. This is a very special day. Just remember that Carolyn looks truly lovely and I am proud that she is keeping her composure. Maxwell will soon be back; Ridley House is only just outside Ashford.'

Only a few minutes passed before they

heard the church door being opened and all gave a sigh of relief.

She knew that she should not have done it, but Carolyn turned her head to look at Edwin, thankful that he was not ill. She received a shock and grasped her father's hand. A rough, loud voice rang through the church.

'Jeremiah Chalke. Bow Street Runner. I've come for Mr Edwin Richard Baillie-Johnson, late of London. Have evidence that he is here to be married today and I arrest him on a charge of embezzlement in the City of London. Would you please step forward, Mr Baillie-Johnson.'

SIX

In the parish church at Ashford, there was a stunned silence; the sounds from the organ had stopped abruptly and Carolyn found that she was holding her breath.

It was Robert who breached the silence; without looking at his sister, he got up from the pew and strode quickly to the back of the church. Carolyn, her head still turned in that direction, saw him confront the intruder. It was then she looked away and heard the horrifying interchange between the two men.

Robert's voice came first. 'I don't know if you are referring to Mr Edwin Baillie who is to be married to my sister in this church today, but if he is indeed the gentleman you seek, then I am afraid that you will be disappointed. Mr Baillie has not, as yet, arrived. Indeed, we are anxiously awaiting his arrival, for he is late.'

The rough voice replied in what seemed to be a tone of some indignation. 'Not here? And calling hisself Mr Baillie? If that ain't just Jeremiah Chalke's luck; missed him again, and me so sure from certain information that I would find him here in this church at eleven o'clock this morning. Not turned up for his own wedding? He had got hold of information that I were after 'im, sure as sure . . . What did you say, sir?'

Robert had said something very quietly and Carolyn could not quite hear what was said even in the quietness of the church.

But there was no mistaking the runner's next words. 'Embezzlement, that's what it is. London firm of attorneys is after him and him no doubt thinking that he was safe here in quiet little Ashford and not using his proper name. Well, if he's not here, I'm off; go and take another look at that flash house of his, might be hiding somewhere, I shouldn't wonder. Knows very well I'll catch up with him sooner or later, he does. There's not much don't escape Jeremiah Chalke. I'll bid you g'day.'

The church door was slammed shut and

the sound echoed throughout the church. Everything seemed to go hazy to Carloyn then and she buried her face in her hands; she felt her father's arms around her shoulders, and heard the sound of her mother's sobs.

Then came the buzz of voices around the church, voices muted with shock, dismay and also with astonishment.

Carolyn heard the church door yet again, but dared not raise her head. She heard Robert speaking to someone and wondered if it could possibly be Edwin.

Edwin? Embezzlement? Bow Street? The words were like a confused roar in her ears and when she at last looked up, she felt the whole church swim round her. *I must not faint, I must not faint,* she was thinking and then she heard the sound of someone calling her own name; it was spoken urgently.

'Carolyn, Carolyn.'

It was Maxwell.

She stood up and without any thought of where she was, she went into his arms and he held her fiercely to him. 'Just come with me, dear girl, we will take you home. Robert is talking to the rector and will make an announcement . . . do you understand, Carolyn? Edwin is not coming; the law is after him. I will explain later, but we must get you home.'

Still with his arm around her, Maxwell turned to Sir William who was trying to calm his hysterical wife; Lizzie sat motionless. 'Sir William, see to Lady Hadleigh and try to explain that there is to be no wedding. I am taking Carolyn home to Ferrers Court . . . Lizzie, you come with us to help Carolyn with her gown.'

As Carolyn walked up the aisle towards the door, Maxwell on one side of her and passing his strength to her and Lizzie holding her arm on the other side, she heard her mother's cry.

'Carolyn . . . my poor girl, and Edwin . . .' There followed a wail. 'Not our good Edwin . . . no, no, I cannot believe it . . . William . . .'

Everything after that became a haze of horror to Carolyn; she remembered being helped into the carriage, she remembered sitting still and upright between Maxwell and Lizzie as though she was frozen stiff with cold. But she had no recall of the journey back to Ferrers Court. The next thing she knew was that Lizzie was helping her off with her gown—the maids were still in the church.

Lizzie, the little girl everyone thought to be silly, was being strong and sensible. She did her best to speak calmly as she laid the wedding gown on the bed and helped Carolyn into a day dress.

'Just sit there, Carolyn. Don't try and move, don't try and think. I am going to fetch you some brandy and a hot drink of tea; that is what you need. It is all such a terrible shock and hard to understand, but I am with you and

Mama and Papa will soon be here.'

Left on her own, Carolyn started to think. She was not married to Edwin. She was home again at Ferrers Court and sitting in her own bedroom. That Edwin had committed some crime and was wanted by the law, that a Bow Street Runner had stopped her wedding to Edwin, she found hard to believe.

I have not married Edwin, I am not married to Edwin, she kept saying to herself and to her astonishment, she felt an enormous relief.

She sobbed then and, as she wiped away her tears, she knew that she was crying because she had not become the wife of a gentleman she did not love. My heart was not involved; I am not hurt. Everyone will think that I am heart-broken, but I am not. It is a relief. Oh, what a fool I have been to think that I could marry a man I did not love and there I was, in my beautiful wedding gown at the altar steps. I do not know what has happened to Edwin, all I know is that I am not his wife . . .

Lizzie returned. She had changed out of her pretty dress while she had been gone and she was forthright as she watched her sister sip the brandy and drink the tea.

'Carolyn, we don't know what Edwin has been up to, but we do know that he must have committed some crime or other. It does not seem possible, not the proper Edwin, but I will be truthful and tell you that I guessed that your heart was not in the match. Oh, I know we all thought that it was suitable and that the two of you dealt very well together, but it was not romantic, was it?'

Carolyn smiled at last at Lizzie's attempts to comfort her. Dear Lizzie was right, she had summed it all up and come to the right conclusion.

'No, Lizzie,' Carolyn said quietly. 'You are quite right. It was very suitable, but it was not romantic. I feel for Mama, Lizzie, is she home yet?'

'I have not heard the carriage,' replied Lizzie. 'But you wait here quietly and drink your tea while I go and watch for them. I am afraid that poor Mama will be having a sad attack of the vapours.'

'Yes,' agreed Carolyn and watched Lizzie go. She was glad to be on her own with her own thoughts.

Carolyn was so wrapped up in those thoughts that she heard nothing of the arrival at Ferrers Court of many carriages and gigs; she did not know that there was a houseful of visitors until the unexpected and somewhat triumphant arrival in her bedroom of an excited Lady Hadleigh.

Carolyn's bedroom was at the back of the house and her window overlooked the vegetable garden and the orchard; beyond that was the wood and in the distance, stretching for mile upon mile towards the sea, was the Marsh. She had a longing to be there now, free of her dresses, on the back of Trixie and galloping alongside the dykes, across the heaths, letting the vast, wild space banish all thoughts of Edwin Baillie.

It should have been my warning, she was thinking, Edwin never liked the Marsh. Granny Harland tried to tell me, but I obstinately went on going what I thought was the right way. She turned suddenly from the window as the door was opened and her mama stood there.

'Oh, Mama,' Carolyn cried out. 'I am sorry, I am very sorry to have put you to so much distress and shame. All the food that you and cook had prepared for the wedding breakfast and now no wedding.'

Lady Hadleigh looked at her daughter searchingly. She had expected to find her red-eyed with weeping. 'You are remarkably calm, my dear,' she said, as she gave Carolyn a kiss.

'I have been thinking, Mama, and Lizzie has been so good to me. But you, Mama, we were expecting you to have an attack of the vapours at the very least. It was so upsetting for you in the church. Do we know yet what has happened to Edwin?'

'One thing at a time, my dear. No, we do not know what Edwin is about or where he is; Robert and Maxwell are with your papa at the moment. But it is quite obvious that you have been saved from a disastrous marriage if a Bow Street Runner had to come after him. I was mortified and shocked in the church in front of the rector and all our friends and our tenants. I thought I should never recover from the ignominy of it all. But Robert and Maxwell have been a tower of strength—there is the gentleman you should have married, Carolyn, Lieutenant Maxwell Forbes. He was so good; going round to Ridley House to find out what had happened to Edwin . . . no, he will tell you in his own good time. Now, where was I?'

Carolyn was beginning to be amused; her mama had spirit. 'The wedding breakfast, Mama?'

Lady Hadleigh nodded. 'Yes, that is right. When Maxwell had taken you and Lizzie from the church, fortunately I had my vinaigrette so I was recovering from the shock of it all. I realized that everyone was still sitting there not knowing what to do. Even your poor father was silent.'

'So what happened.'

'I got up on my feet and faced them all. I did not know that I had the courage to do such a thing. "Friends", I said and quite boldly, "this is a sad day for poor Carolyn as well as being a scandal. We came here to celebrate a wedding and then to repair to Ferrers Court for the wedding breakfast. We have not had a wedding and we have no bridegroom, but the wedding breakfast awaits us and I hope you will all return to enjoy our hospitality and to commiserate with our poor daughter. I do not expect her to appear before you all, but I am sure that this would be her wish." That is what I said, Carolyn, and I hope that I did the right thing.'

'You mean that . . .' Carolyn could not finish.

'I mean that they are all arriving and are enjoying the food and the wine and having a good gossip about Mr Edwin Baillie. I know that you will wish to be quiet, but I hope that you will let me send up a little refreshment for you. Lizzie will bring it and stay with you.'

Carolyn gave her mama a hug. 'You have been splendid, Mama, and you have done the right thing. I will come down later and perhaps Robert and Maxwell will be able to tell me about Edwin.'

'You are not heart-broken?' Lady Hadleigh said suddenly.

Carolyn smiled. 'No, not heart-broken. I realize that my heart was not really in the match though I was fond of Edwin. I will soon forget him, you know. It was a case of the head ruling the heart rather than the other way round.'

'I am glad to hear it, though I liked Edwin. It shows how mistaken one can be in a person. Perhaps the lieutenant, my dear—' She was not allowed to finish.

'No, Mama,' came firmly from Carolyn. 'You need not start match-making on my account. It will be a long time—if ever—

before I walk up the aisle in a wedding gown again; perhaps I will become an old maid and be a fond aunt to Robert and Lizzie's children.'

'But, Carolyn . . .'

'No, Mama, no match-making. Please go and welcome our guests and give my apologies. I am sure that they will understand if I do not appear; it will give them something to talk about!'

'Very well, my dear.' Lady Hadleigh kissed Carolyn and sailed from the room as though she was going off to enjoy the scandal of it all now that she knew that she did not have a heart-broken daughter on her hands.

Carolyn smiled and stood at the window again, thinking of what had occurred and wishing that she knew more of what had happened to Edwin. It was true that her heart was not broken, but she was intrigued.

Lizzie brought her a tray of food and some wine and, together, they enjoyed the little feast; Carolyn found, somewhat to her astonishment, that she was hungry.

'Robert and Maxwell are still with Papa,' said Lizzie. 'I wonder what it is all about? Do you know what embezzlement is, Carolyn? Is it really a crime?'

'I believe it means to use money that has been entrusted to you—for safe-keeping that is—for your own purposes. Especially if it is the money which rightfully belongs to your

94

employer or your partner in business. In Edwin's case, I should think it must have been the attorneys who were his associates when he was in London.'

Lizzie wrinkled her nose. 'Oh, I see, or I think I do. Is it a very serious crime? Would Edwin have to go to prison?'

'I don't know, Lizzie, I really do not know a lot about it, but I expect that Papa will tell us soon.'

It was not long after this that she was summoned to the library and she succeeded in avoiding most of the guests who filled the drawing-room and the dining-room.

Her father was looking very serious, but he took her hand as though to try and reassure her.

'Carolyn, my dear, this is all very unfortunate and I feel most sorry. I also feel somewhat guilty as I had approved of Edwin and thought him an excellent prospect. He had told me that he was studying in the law and hoped eventually to become a barrister. So his prospects were good and his manner was very correct. He was obviously very fond of you and I had no hesitation in giving my consent to the match.' He stopped speaking and looked very thoughtful. 'But I should have been warned by one thing.'

Carolyn frowned. 'What do you mean, Papa?'

'Edwin was most particular in wanting to

know the details of the marriage settlement. He knew that I am a very wealthy man and that I would do well for you. He even insisted on me naming the sum I would settle on you when you married him.'

Carolyn spoke in a hushed voice. 'Was it a lot of money, Papa?'

He nodded soberly. 'It ran into some thousands of pounds, my dear; I wanted to be assured of your comfort.'

'Do you mean that Edwin was probably wanting to marry me for my money?' she asked.

'I cannot be sure, but from what Robert and Maxwell have told me, it begins to look like it. I am sorry, Carolyn, very sorry. I blame myself.'

'It is all right, Papa, I want to know the truth. What did Maxwell find out when he kindly went in search of Edwin?'

Sir William put his hand on her arm. 'I will leave the lieutenant to tell you himself. He did not mention all the details to me. There is a fine young gentleman, Carolyn.'

She smiled at him. 'Not you too, Papa!'

'What do you mean, my child?'

'Mama is trying to match-make with Edwin hardly out of the door. I have vowed to be an old maid.'

Back in her room and now on her own as Lizzie had joined the guests downstairs, Carolyn was very thoughtful.

So Edwin had been relying on her inheritance when he had asked her to marry him. In many ways, this did not come as a shock to her; rather, it explained one or two things that he had said to her which had puzzled her at the time.

She searched her memory. How he said once, 'I expect it will all work out for the best' or some such thing when she had refused to marry him until Robert was home. She remembered now that he had been quite put out because she would not agree to marry him immediately.

Then on another occasion when he had been urging her to name the day and she had said that she was not sure that she wished for the marriage, she had been mystified at his reply, 'You must marry me, everything depends on it'. On the same occasion, she had been surprised at the keen ardour for her which he had never shown before and she had told him so. He had replied that one day she would understand. She remembered saying that she would cry off and his reply had been that he must have her. Surely that should have warned her?

Finally, when Robert had returned and she agreed to rush their wedding, he had shown such obvious relief, 'Thank God', he had said.

Had she been a fool? No, she told herself now, she was used to dealing with honest people and it had never occurred to her that

Edwin was anything but honest.

It was Robert who interrupted her thoughts. He tapped on the door and stood in the doorway.

'I am so sorry, sister dear,' he said. 'But I do believe that you have had a lucky escape. Now I hate to have to tell you this, but Maxwell and I have to leave within the hour. I will say goodbye to you now as we have agreed that it should be Maxwell who will tell you as much as he has learned about Edwin. He says that if you are fit enough, he will walk with you in the garden. It is fine and sunny, but you will need your pelisse. Are you agreeable?'

Carolyn could only feel gladness. She wanted to know the truth and she wanted to bid farewell to Maxwell and to thank him for his help.

She went up to Robert and kissed him. 'Thank you, Robert, I will come and see Maxwell and then I will wave you off. Have most of the guests gone now?'

He nodded. 'Yes, only Uncle George and Aunt Prim are still here and I think that they go tomorrow, you will find them most sympathetic.'

She became serious. 'I wish you well, Robert. You will be a full lieutenant now. God keep you safe. Please write to us when you have the opportunity: I cannot begin to tell you how much your letters mean to us.'

Robert hugged her. 'I am proud of you.

Many young ladies would have collapsed in the circumstances.'

She smiled. 'I am made of sterner stuff, Robert,' she told him, and they both of them laughed.

Maxwell was standing in the hall when she went downstairs and he gripped her hand. 'I am sorry, Carolyn, that is all that I can say. It is not something one would wish to happen to any young lady, but Robert says that you told him that you are made of stern stuff!'

She smiled. 'And so I am. Shall we walk in the garden?'

'We seem destined to meet in your shrubbery,' he said teasingly. 'I am beginning to think that it is a dangerous place for our emotions.'

As they walked away from the house, Carolyn was remembering their previous disturbing encounters in the shrubbery, but she made no reply to him. This was to be a farewell and Maxwell would be telling her of Edwin and giving her the explanation of that young gentleman's extraordinary behaviour. Robert had been right about the weather, it was now mid-afternoon, the sun was shining and for September, it held a lot of warmth. Carolyn was glad of that warmth as she sat on the seat at Maxwell's side.

'I know that you are anxious to hear what happened when I went in search of Edwin,' he said quietly. 'Are you prepared for a long story?'

SEVEN

In the quiet garden, Carolyn braced herself for what was to be revealed to her concerning the man she had planned to marry.

'Yes, I am prepared, Maxwell, I know the enormity of it all, but none of the details. Tell me exactly what you did when you went in search of Edwin.'

'I took the gig—Robert and I had used the gig to get to the church, you know—and drove straight to Ridley House. I think I expected to find Edwin stricken with a sudden illness. The place was deserted. The front door barred, the back door bolted. Not a soul about the place, no one to be seen anywhere. I went round to the stables and it was the same story. No curricle, no gig and certainly no sign of the carriage which he is supposed to have acquired to take you into Cornwall. Neither was there any sign of a stable boy or coachman. It was all quite deserted, as I said. I went back to my gig. I was at a standstill and had to think hard. I was also in a rush as I kept thinking of you waiting in the church. Little did I know that you had had a visit from a Bow Street Runner at that stage, though of course, I found out later.'

'When he came into the church,' Carolyn told him, 'I thought it was you coming back with Edwin. It was such a dreadful shock hearing his words, but of course you did not return until he had left. Where had you been, Maxwell?'

'I stood with the gig outside Ridley House trying to decide what to do next. Should I come back and tell you that the place was locked up? But then I remembered you once telling me the name of the attorneys with whom Edwin worked in Ashford—Cullen, Clarke and Cullen or something like that. I decided to go and see if they knew of Edwin's wherabouts.' He paused and looked at her.

'It is quite a long story, Carolyn and I am afraid that it will shock you, but I will make it as short as I can. The partners at Cullen's were in a state of disorganization, partly from shock. They had just received a visit from Jeremiah Chalke, Bow Street Runner, and had learned that Edwin was wanted for embezzlement in connection with the firm he was with in London. He had pocketed a lot of funds dishonestly and when they caught up with him, he had fled. We now know that he had changed his name and made his way to Ashford. Cullen's began to be suspicious when he purchased Ridley House, but they could not prove anything; then they discovered that he was to receive a generous marriage settlement from Sir William Hadleigh and they were

101

satisfied. Did you know of the settlement, Carolyn?' he asked suddenly.

'Papa told me a little while ago, and when I came to think it over, I realized that Edwin was relying on the money coming to him. He kept on urging me to marry him quickly and absolutely insisted on it being during Robert's time at home.' She paused and was thoughtful. 'So what happened at Cullen's?'

'In the short time that it took Jeremiah Chalke to reach the church and for me to go to Ridley House and then on to their office, they had made a frantic search through their books and discovered many discrepancies. Some of them were large sums of money. I did not stay to hear any more and came back to you as quickly as I could.'

Maxwell turned to her and took her hands. 'I am sorry, my dear; were you very fond of Edwin? I ask you that, though I think that I know the answer.'

'No, Maxwell, you do not know entirely, though I tried to explain when we were sitting in this very place last night . . . what a lot has happened since then!' Carolyn managed to give a little laugh. 'I *was* fond of Edwin, but I never suspected that he had a dishonest side to his nature. That has come as a shocking revelation. I think the biggest shock of the day has been not the non-appearance of Edwin, but the arrival in the church of the Bow Street Runner. What will happen if Edwin is caught,

Maxwell?'

'He will be tried, presumably found guilty and probably sent to the Marshalsea,' he replied.

'That is the debtor's prison?' she asked.

He nodded. 'Yes, and he will find himself with many a respectable gentleman who has taken up residence there.'

'You know all about it, Maxwell,' she said with a smile.

'I think there are a few naval people amongst the debtors,' he observed. 'Now, to be serious, having got the subject of Edwin Baillie's misdemeanours out of the way: you have no regrets, Carolyn?'

She sighed. 'It has all been such a shock, but I can see now that my heart was not really engaged in it all. I will soon make a recovery. Is it time for you and Robert to go, Maxwell?'

'Not quite, it is an easy journey, straight along the south coast. Robert knows that I am saying goodbye to you.'

Carolyn looked serious. 'Does it not alarm you, Maxwell, knowing that you are going to be with Lord Nelson in order to try and defeat the combined fleet?'

'Alarm me? Damme, I am a naval officer, Carolyn: we face death at every turn. There is no room for alarm or fear. I came through the Battle of the Nile when I was only a midshipman and I have been with Lord Nelson ever since; there was the Battle of

Copenhagen, too, but that was nearly four years ago. We *must* defeat Napoleon on the seas, dear girl. We have to make our small island safe, you know. Who could choose to serve with other than Lord Nelson, though there is also Collingwood, of course.'

'You admire the vice-admiral,' she said, and knew she need not ask the question.

'We trust him, Carolyn, he is a great man. I know that he is a gentleman of small stature and he is getting frail; he has lost an arm, he is blind in one eye, but still he commands the fleet and his men trust him, as I say. Then, be it right or wrong, he still commands the love of Lady Hamilton.'

She looked at him with some curiosity; everyone knew of the vice-admiral's scandalous affair with the wife of Sir William Hamilton when that gentleman had been ambassador in Naples. Since then, the pair had set up an establishment together near London and had a small child whom Lord Nelson called his 'godchild'.

'Have you met Lady Hamilton?' she asked Maxwell. 'Is she really very beautiful?'

He nodded. 'Only last week,' he told her. 'Robert and I drove out to their house in Merton. It is the grandest place; in Lord Nelson's absence, Lady Hamilton has busied herself decorating it. I have never seen anything quite like it. The whole house, staircase and all, are covered with pictures of them both, representations of his naval actions, coats of arms, pieces of plate; it all seemed to be in very bad taste, but how is one to judge? We were made very welcome and had a splendid dinner, with Lady Hamilton sitting at the head of the table and her mother, Mrs Cadogan, at the bottom; Lord Nelson was most genial amongst his family. But that is enough about our great commander of the fleet: what about us, Carolyn?'

'We have to say goodbye,' she replied soberly, and her thoughts were sober, too. What a strange day it had been; she had expected to be on her way to Cornwall with her new husband, the gentleman of her choice, and here she was saying farewell to the naval lieutenant whom she knew she was near to loving.

'I don't know when I will be back again, Carolyn. Will you still be here? Will you wait for me?'

They looked at each other and there was understanding in their eyes: Carolyn knew what was being left unsaid.

'Yes, Maxwell, I will wait,' she said quietly.

'Thank you,' was all he said, and he leaned forward and his lips touched hers very gently, softly and with a hint of promise.

He got up and walked away from her, back into the house. She watched him go and knew that she had lost and gained all in the space of a few hours.

They all waved Robert and Maxwell off and after the pair had gone, Carolyn felt tired and exhausted. She managed to get through dinner with her aunt and uncle and cousins, but afterwards, Lady Hadleigh, seeing the look of strain on her daughter's face, sent her straight off to bed.

Carolyn was astonished to find that she slept well and when she awoke, her first thoughts were of Maxwell and not of Edwin. They have both gone out of my life, she thought. It will seem strange not to have Edwin calling almost every day, but I think I will soon forget him.

She knew that this was because of the person of Lieutenant Maxwell Forbes and of that gentleman's power over her feelings. I must not dwell upon him, she told herself, it is possible that I might never see him again.

At breakfast, she was pleased to see that her mama and Aunt Prim were in cheerful mood and that they had been hatching a plot for her immediate future.

'Carolyn,' said her mother in greeting. 'I trust that you have slept well after all the shocks and disappointments of yesterday. It would seem that you were saved from being married to a scoundrel in the nick of time and we must give thanks for that. Now, your Aunt Prim and I have been talking and she has made what I consider a very sensible suggestion.'

106

Younger than Lady Hadleigh, Aunt Prim had married George Hadleigh when she had been only eighteen years of age. George was Sir William's junior, but the two brothers had always been close. George owned and managed a small estate in the village of Upper Hardres near Canterbury. From Ferrers Court, it was easily reached along the old Roman road of Stone Street which ran in an almost straight line from Canterbury to Aldington. Thus the two families had always been close and Carolyn was fond of her aunt and uncle and her two cousins.

Aunt Prim sounded enthusiastic that morning. 'Yes, Carolyn, I want to ask if you would like to come back to Upper Hardres to stay with us for a little while. I know that Jane and Mary are much younger than you, but you know them well and you have always enjoyed your visits to Pettes House. I have another reason though for asking you to come. In many ways, it is asking you to help us out, but I hope that you will not mind.'

Carolyn was intrigued; perhaps it would be good to have something to think of other than the scapegrace Edwin and the handsome Maxwell.

Her aunt continued. 'We have staying with us a young lady from the village who is in great distress. Her name is Cecily Burns and she is just a little younger than you. She has had an unfortunate life, for her mother died when she was born and she has no brothers or sisters. She was brought up by her father, who, I regret to say, admirable gentleman though he was—he was a great scholar—regarded Cecily more as a servant to his needs than as a daughter. Now he has died and, as they have no immediate family, we have taken her into our own home where she is most welcome to stay until we can perhaps find a suitor for her. I am taking a long time to reach what I wish to ask you, but I expect you can guess! I think it would help Cecily a lot to be in your company; she is fond of riding and I know that is a favourite pastime of yours. We can find you a mount easily: Jane and Mary have never had a liking for horses, but your uncle keeps a good stable. Now, tell me what you think of the idea.'

Carolyn felt nothing but delight. 'I would love to come, Aunt Prim, and thank you very much for asking me. I am sure that I could soon make a good friend of Cecily especially if she is fond of horses.'

They talked of their plans all through breakfast and, as Uncle George wished to return that very day, Carolyn and Lizzie were sent off to pack a portmanteau with everything which would be needed for a short stay.

They reached Upper Hardres later that same day and Carolyn was taken into the house to meet Cecily Burns. The two girls liked each other straight away and both had a tale to tell. Cecily sat on the bed while Carolyn unpacked the portmanteau, she having declined the services of Aunt Prim's only maid.

Cecily was bursting with curiosity for she knew very well that the Hadleighs had gone off to Aldington to their niece's wedding.

Carolyn thought her a very pretty girl in the sense that she was small and neat, with dark curls and blue eyes, though it dismayed her to see such a young lady dressed all in black.

'I am very sorry to hear of your sad loss, Cecily, but I am glad that you have come to stay with my Aunt Prim and that you are not entirely on your own.'

Cecily managed a sweet smile. 'It is so kind of Mrs Hadleigh to bring you here as company for me. She has told me that you like to ride which is very nice for me as it is one of my favourite pastimes. Mary and Jane are dear girls, but they do not like horses and I am not allowed to ride out on my own. But, Carolyn, you were to be married and I cannot wait to ask you what has happened. It has made me very curious, so I hope that you do not mind me asking you about it.'

'No, of course not,' Carolyn replied. 'To tell you the truth, I can hardly believe it, for it happened only yesterday. But I thought it was a lovely idea to come here with aunt and uncle, especially when they told me of your troubles.'

'Are you not upset at what happened at your wedding? Mrs Hadleigh did tell me about it briefly.'

Carolyn smiled. 'And you cannot wait to hear the whole story! There, that is the last of my dresses, we will both of us sit on the bed and I will tell you the tale. It is quite shocking and you will wonder at my lack of sensibility.'

'We will see,' was all of Cecily's reply.

So the tale was told and Carolyn saw both shock and sympathy in Cecily's eyes. 'So there you are,' she concluded. 'My husband-to-be is on his way to the Marshalsea if Mr Jeremiah Chalke has succeeded in catching up with him.'

'You make so light of it,' was Cecily's comment. 'To be left at the altar was a dreadful thing to happen to a young lady, but I suppose we must think that you had a lucky escape. Can one be so easily deceived in a person, Carolyn? Did you love Edwin very much?'

Carolyn was silent for a moment, then considered her reply carefully. 'I respected him as a gentleman and as a lawyer, I cannot say more than that. I know that I did not love him in the way that novels talk about love, but I did not regard that as a hindrance to a good marriage. I thought it was the respect that mattered.'

'What about the lieutenant?'

Carolyn started. 'Why should you ask such a question?'

Cecily gave a smile. 'I thought that I could

110

detect something in your voice when you told me how he had gone to find Edwin for you.'

'I will confess I *do* like Lieutenant Forbes and I was sad to have to say goodbye to him, but as I will probably never see him again, I must forget him.'

'I think you are very brave,' said Cecily. 'The way you have come here to be with me after such a dreadful thing happening to you. I should be consoling you!'

Carolyn laughed. 'Perhaps we will be good for each other,' she said and became more serious. 'Tell me about your father, Cecily. I am very sorry and offer my sincere condolences.'

'Thank you, it is kind of you. Poor Papa, he was such a dear and I loved him, but he lived in a world of his own. You have to understand that he was not a young man when he married my mother and was over forty years of age when he was left with a young baby. But he would not give me up even though I had cousins in Scotland who would have taken me. He loved Mama so much and I was all he had left. So he had nursemaids and my dear Mrs Roddick to keep house for him. She was heart-broken when he died and the house was sold and she has gone to live with her daughter.'

'But you, Cecily, did you not have a governess?' Carolyn asked.

Cecily smiled. 'Papa was my governess! He was very learned, you know. He had studied archaeology at Oxford and his head was in the past. He had a small income from his father's estate and we lived very frugally. But he taught me all the English and history and geography I needed to know and he had so much patience with me. Then when our lessons were over, he would shut himself in his study and I would not see him until dinner.'

'It was a lonely life for you,' observed Carolyn.

'I suppose it was, but I have always had the Hadleigh family nearby and they kindly let me go riding as long as I had a stable boy with me and I was never short of friends. But do you know, Carolyn, I have become so learned myself that I am thinking of applying for a post as a governess.'

For a moment, Carolyn was shocked. 'But you are a lady, Cecily; a governess is little more than a servant.' She paused. 'No, perhaps I am wrong. We have Miss Grimble at home and she is more like one of the family. She taught Robert and me—Robert is my older brother and he is with Lord Nelson on board the *Victory*—and now we have two little ones in the schoolroom, Ben and Lucy. There is also Lizzie, she is just sixteen and you would like her. She is very pretty, not a bit like me!'

'But you are lovely, Carolyn. With your dark hair and dark eyes, I think that you are very striking.'

Carolyn laughed ruefully. 'I think I had

112

rather be beautiful than striking, but one cannot choose one's looks.'

The visit was an extremely successful one. The two girls rode every day and the countryside was a refreshing change; the village of Upper Hardres was prettily sited, high above sea-level, with fine views over the distant Kent countryside. She missed the Marsh, but she was enjoying the pleasing company of Cecily Burns.

She returned to Aldington and Ferrers Court at the beginning of October. The days were becoming colder and Carolyn felt the need for her warmer day dresses. She was sad to say goodbye to Cecily, but promised that she would go to Upper Hardres again in the spring.

Cecily laughingly said that she would probably be far away by that time, being a governess to some naughty, spoiled children. They parted with a kiss and a vow to write to each other.

Carolyn soon settled down at home again and within a week of her being back at Ferrers Court came a letter from Robert. They had guessed that the *Victory* had joined the fleet somewhere near Spain and the country was anxiously awaiting news.

She took the precious letter up to her bedroom so that she could savour it quietly to herself. She wondered if there would be any mention of Maxwell, for he was often in her thoughts even though she tried hard to forget their moments together and their last words out in the shrubbery.

off Spain, September 1805

My dear family
I had not expected to have the chance of writing to you so soon, but it so happens that poor Admiral Calder is being sent home to face a court martial and we have the opportunity of sending letters. You may remember that I told you that Calder commanded a squadron at El Ferrol on the north coast of Spain. He encountered Villeneuve and the French fleet on their return from the West Indies, but the action was unsatisfactory and Calder was injured. Now it seems he is to be reprimanded for it. The combined fleet is blockaded in Cadiz harbour, but I have no doubt that Lord Nelson will entice them out and we shall see some action. The weather off this treacherous and exposed coast is atrocious, with gales and bitter winds.
I end with my own very good news. As soon as I boarded the Victory *at Portsmouth and presented my certificate, Lord Nelson himself promoted me to the rank of lieutenant. Maxwell is proud of my success and is still my staunchest friend. He sends his regards to you and his love to*

Carolyn. I am not sure if this means anything, but Carolyn will know.
Your loving son Robert

Carolyn read the letter time and time again. Was Maxwell just being affectionate towards her or did his brief message have a deeper meaning? But she treasured the words and would always remember him with love.

Another letter was received at about this time. It was to Sir William, and came from Cullen, Clarke and Cullen giving them further news of Edwin. Her father gave it to Carolyn to read for herself.

Dear Sir William
I write with reference to our former colleague, Mr Edwin Baillie. It is with deep regret that I have to confess that we did not keep a closer eye on the finances in the firm. There has never been any suspicion of wrong-doing in financial matters and so our affairs were not sufficiently questioned.

Had we kept a closer eye on these matters, Mr Baillie would not have been able to rob us of sufficient money to buy Ridley House. The embezzlement took place in such a clever and underhand way that until Mr Jeremiah Chalke appeared on our doorstep, we had trusted Mr Baillie implicitly.

We have since learned from a firm of

*London attorneys that he had used the
same practices in their employ and thought
that by escaping to Ashford he would evade
the law. As far as I know, he still eludes the
Bow Street Runner.*

*Lastly, I would like to extend my regrets
to your daughter on what should have been
her wedding day; however, we must be
thankful that she has had a fortunate
escape from a man who proved to be
nothing but a thief and a rascal.*

I remain your servant, sir . . .

Carolyn smiled at these last words; to her,
to describe the very proper Edwin as a thief
and a rascal was nothing short of comical.
Perhaps that is how I must remember him, she
told herself, it is right to say that it was a lucky
escape.

EIGHT

It seemed a long time to Carolyn since her last
visit to Granny Harland and much had
happened in that time. She had no doubt that
Granny would have heard of the scandal
surrounding Edwin and of the events of
Carolyn's wedding day.

It was a quiet, flat morning when she rode
across the Marsh, the clouds were low and

threatened rain and the greyness of it added to the unique marshland atmosphere.

Carolyn rode quietly, too, savouring the flat, open space of it all, the distant horizon of the sea; sometimes the Marsh asked her to go quietly, sometimes the wind would howl and beg her to gallop.

'Oh, Miss Car'lyn,' said Granny Harland, when Carolyn reached the cottage. 'And here's me been longing for a sight of you to say I'm sorry for all the trouble you've been in.'

'I would have come before, Granny,' said Carolyn, as she gave the old lady a kiss, 'but after the wedding that wasn't a wedding, I went back with my Aunt and Uncle Hadleigh and stayed with them near Canterbury for a week or two. But we have received a letter from Robert and I thought you would like me to read it to you.'

'Thank you, Miss Car'lyn, thank you. Now is it to be milk or small ale today?'

'I'll have some milk, thank you.'

Granny Harland was eager to hear the gossip. 'So all that heart-searching you had over Mr Edwin came to nothing then. I tried to tell you the best way I could the last time you was here, but I had the feeling all the time that he weren't the one for you. Seems I were right.'

'He turned out to be a scoundrel, Granny, but I never would have suspected it. He was so very proper, but perhaps that should have warned me.'

'You did what you thought were the right thing, Miss Car'lyn, even if your heart were telling you otherwise. You was lucky you found out about'n when you did, even if it were in the church on the very day of your wedding. I never heard such a thing, I never did; a wedding being stopped by a Bow Street Runner. 'Tis a pity no one found a pediment or whatever they call it when the banns was called.'

Carolyn laughed heartily. 'You are quite right, Granny, you always will be right, I know that for certain. There is not a nicer or wiser person on the Marsh than you.'

'That's as maybe. 'Tis only common sense is what I say. So you're not married after all. Have you got another young gentleman in mind then?'

Carolyn was not honest. 'I will be an old maid, Granny,' was all she said.

'Rubbish,' pronounced Granny Harland. 'You'll be snapped up in no time at all, you mark my words and you just come an tell old Granny when you've found the person who you can love and who loves you. That's what I'll be waiting to hear, and, Miss Car'lyn, make sure as it's someone as loves the Marsh this time.'

Carolyn rode back to Ferrers Court cheered by the visit; she knew that she would remember Granny Harland's words.

118

At the end of October, there was at Ferrers Court a small crisis. It came as a blow to them all, but was soon resolved.

Miss Grimble, the children's governess, was now fifty years of age and much loved. She had been with the family for twenty years. Ashford born and bred, in all those years it had been her custom, on her afternoon off, to visit her sister Marjorie in the town. Marjorie was older than she was, married and with a family who had all themselves married and left home. Marjorie's husband, Tom, would bring their small gig to Aldington to fetch Miss Grimble every Wednesday afternoon and then bring her back again in the evening.

Tom had been failing for many years and it did not come as a surprise to the Hadleigh family when he died suddenly of an attack to the heart.

Sir William took Miss Grimble to her sister, who was almost prostrate with grief. Later the governess had to tell Lady Hadleigh that she was very sorry but she could not return to Ferrers Court. Marjorie needed her and that was her place.

The children and Lizzie cried as she left with all her luggage and Carolyn felt very sad. That night, she and her mother talked about how they should go about getting a new governess and Carolyn had a suggestion to make.

'Mama, I told you about Cecily Burns who is

staying with Aunt Prim and Uncle George at the moment; she has been left sadly alone and has very little to support her, for her father was a scholar and not a rich man. Cecily was well educated by him and now talks of becoming a governess in order to support herself. Do you think we could give her a chance with Ben and Lucy? I would like to help her and it seems an opportunity not to be missed. What do you think?'

'How old is she, Carolyn?' Lady Hadleigh asked thoughtfully.

'She is my age, but she is a very sensible girl and not a silly young miss. I think that she could do it and I think Ben and Lucy would love her.'

Lady Hadleigh made up her mind quickly. 'I will write to her. It can do no harm in giving her a chance and I like what you say of her. Prim and George have been very kind, but it would be a relief to them to see her settled, I am sure.'

Carolyn was delighted. 'Thank you, Mama, thank you very much.'

The letter was written and a week later in the darker days as November approached, Uncle George Hadleigh brought Cecily to Ferrers Court.

Cecily was so grateful that when she saw Carolyn the tears ran down her face, then she hastily brushed them away and gave a smile. 'It is so good of you to think of me, Carolyn, I will do my very best.'

'Come up to the schoolroom and meet the children. They have been having a holiday since Miss Grimble left, but I have been sitting with them every day to hear them read and help them with their writing.'

Cecily looked a little fearful. 'What subjects would Lady Hadleigh like me to teach them?' she asked.

'Just the usual things,' Carolyn replied. 'Apart from their reading and writing which is the most important, things like the use of the globes and the Kings and Queens of England. Oh, and I think Miss Grimble did some nature study, too. I remember when Lizzie and I were small, Miss Grimble used to take us on nature walks; she seemed to know the name of every flower, and butterflies, too. Will you be able to do that?'

Cecily nodded. 'Yes, I think so. Papa was very keen on botany; we used to walk over the fields sometimes when he could tear himself away from his books. Dear Papa, he is at peace now.'

Carolyn took Cecily to the bedroom which was to be hers, then showed her the little sitting-room leading from it which Miss Grimble had always used.

'Cecily, this is Miss Grimble's sitting-room, but Mama and I have discussed it and have both agreed that we wish you to be one of the family. You are near to Lizzie and me in age and we want you to join us at dinner, then spend the evenings in the drawing-room with us.'

Cecily seemed alarmed. 'But I do not expect that; it is not usual for a governess to—join the family.'

'It is not usual for a governess to be a lady with your family history!' Carolyn replied.

They both laughed, Cecily agreed and Carolyn said that the next thing was to meet the children.

'But before we go to the schoolroom,' Carolyn said firmly, 'there is one thing I want to settle between us, and with no argument.'

'Whatever do you mean?' Cecily asked.

'It is your black dresses. You must not be offended by what I am going to say, I know what is proper just as you do. You are in mourning for your father and etiquette requires you to be in black, so you are quite correct, but I have two things to say on the subject and I hope we will not quarrel over it.'

'You don't want me to wear black,' Cecily said, calmly.

Carolyn nodded. 'I do not think it is necessary. First of all, you are too young to be entirely in black and secondly, I do not want the children to have a governess who is always dressed in black . . . no, don't interrupt. Wait until you hear what I have to say. I want to take you into Ashford and we will buy some grey crêpe from the linen-drapers; then we will take it to Miss Hargreaves who is our dressmaker. She will make you up some dresses in no time at all, pretty ones—no frills, but not too plain. It will be quite proper for you to be in grey. Don't you think it is a good idea? Mama and I talked about it before you came and she agrees with me. There is another thing, too, Cecily; grey will suit you with your lovely blue eyes.'

The blue eyes filled with tears, but Cecily did not cry. 'You are too good to me, you and your mama, but I agree with you about the black. I never liked it though I knew it to be correct. It is three months now since Papa died so I think I can safely go into grey. Thank you very much, Carolyn.'

'Good,' Carolyn said briskly. 'That is settled. Now we must go and introduce you to Ben and Lucy.'

The schoolroom was small but pleasant and had the same view of the gardens and the Marsh as was obtained from Carolyn's bedroom.

Two bright-eyed children were playing a game of Snap with Patty, the maid. They jumped up in excitement when they saw their sister with Cecily.

'Ben and Lucy, this is Miss Burns; she is to be your new governess.'

'But she isn't old,' said Benjamin.

Carolyn and Cecily smiled at him, but there was no reprimand and the introductions were made.

'This is Benjamin, who is nine years old and we usually call him Ben; and this is Lucy who is seven.'

Both children looked solemn and shook hands with Cecily who was smiling at them.

'Tell me what Miss Grimble has been teaching you and what you like best,' she said to them.

Neither of them were shy and Carolyn was proud of them.

'I like stories of the kings and queens,' said Ben. 'Specially about Henry VIII, he had six wives and two of them were beheaded.'

Carolyn and Cecily exchanged glances. 'Did Miss Grimble teach you that?' Cecily asked.

'Oh, yes, and lots about the other kings as well. Some were good and some were bad,' he said readily.

'Queen Elizabeth was good,' announced Lucy, not to be left out. 'And I know where Egypt is and that is where Lord Nelson fought a big battle—on the sea, I mean. He has his own ship—'

Ben chipped in. 'It is called the *Victory* and our brother Robert is on the *Victory* and he has been made a left . . . left . . . I've forgotten the proper word.'

'Lieutenant,' said Carolyn and felt proud of them.

They went downstairs then and Cecily was hesitant as they went into the drawing-room.

'It is going to be hard to follow Miss Grimble,' she said forlornly.

'Nonsense, you will do very well. There is one thing in which you have the advantage over Miss Grimble,' Carolyn told her.

'What is that?'

'Miss Grimble disliked horses and could not ride, so the children always had one of the stable boys to take them out on their ponies. Now we will find a nice mare for you and you will be able to go with them.'

Cecily smiled. 'It is all too good to be true and I do thank you, Carolyn.'

It did not take Cecily very long to settle in at Ferrers Court and Carolyn was glad of the company of the young governess whenever Cecily was not involved with the children.

If Lizzie felt left out, she did not complain and was happy as long as she had Gilly, her pony, and was allowed to ride as far as Hollies Farm where the Selhurst family lived. Jenny Selhurst was the same age as Lizzie and for a time, both girls had joined for their lessons with Miss Grimble.

During those last days of October, as they suffered their first frosts and the trees gradually turned to red and gold, the only news to reach the Hadleigh family and the nation at large was not of Lord Nelson and the fleet, but of Napoleon's victory at the battle of Ulm in Bavaria. It was known that the Emperor was harrying the Austrians under

125

General Mack from pillar to post along the Danube, but such an overwhelming victory by Napoleon at Ulm was a stunning blow to Pitt and the British people. They knew they were still vulnerable along their southern coast and every day they looked for Nelson's strike against the combined fleet which was still blockaded in Cadiz harbour.

October wore itself out and November dawned as the herald of winter. It was on the sixth day of that month that news came from the Mediterranean which brought joy, triumph and sorrow in its wake.

Admiral Collingood's dispatch was published in *The Times* of 7 November and the whole country read of the great battle out in the Atlantic off Cape Trafalgar. Lord Nelson, attacking the enemy with the unusual formation of two lines of his fighting ships, crippled the combined fleet and, at last, Emperor Napoleon was defeated. But at such a price, the Hadleigh family read, for Vice-Admiral Lord Nelson had been killed in the great battle.

The nation wept rather than rejoiced and Admiral Collingwood paid his own tribute to the great man in his dispatch; he had written it on 22 October after the battle of the previous day and it had been entrusted to the schooner *Pickle* which took two weeks to reach the Cornish port of Falmouth.

In the drawing-room at Ferrers Court, there

was a dreadful silence; each knew what the other was thinking.

'Oh, what of poor Robert?' Lady Hadleigh cried out. 'We do not even know if he is still alive. Oh, what shall we do?'

In a rare gesture, Sir William put his arm around his wife's shoulders. We must have hope, my dear. It is a terrible thing not to know if our son is alive or not, so there is only hope and patience left to us. There will be so many families feeling just as we do. Read Admiral Collingwood's words and his great tribute to Lord Nelson.'

The newspaper was passed from one to another; none of them had a dry eye on reading it, and Carolyn thought not only of Robert, but of Maxwell too. The words seemed to dance in front of her eyes which were blurred with tears.

> . . . *such a battle could not be fought without sustaining a great loss of men. I have not only to lament in common with the British Navy, and the British Nation, in the fall of the Commander in Chief, the loss of a Hero, whose name will be immortal, and his memory ever dear to his country; but my heart is rent with grief for the death of a friend to whom, by many years of intimacy, and a perfect knowledge of the virtues of his mind, which inspired ideas superior to the common race of men,*

I was bound by the strongest ties of affection; a grief to which even the glorious occasion in which he fell, does not bring the consolation which perhaps it ought; his Lordship received a musket ball in his left breast, about the middle of the action, and sent an officer to me immediately with his last farewell; and soon after expired.

I fear the numbers that have fallen will be found very great, when the returns come to me; but it having blown a gale of wind ever since the action, I have not yet had it in my power to collect any reports from the ships.

'How soon can we expect to have news of Robert?' asked Lady Hadleigh fearfully.

'It is quite possible, my dear,' replied her husband, 'that letters from the men may have been brought by the same schooner as brought the dispatch. Let us hope to hear within a few days, but you must be prepared for it to be a message from the Navy Office. If our Robert has been killed in the battle, then we must always remember him with pride. Such a victory over the combined fleets of France and Spain brings both triumph and sorrow. Without his fleet, Napoleon will never invade the English coast, but it is at a terrible price for we have lost Lord Nelson and we can only pray that Robert is safe.'

And Maxwell, thought Carolyn. They were both of them very dear to her.

The family were fortunate in not having to wait very long for the joy of receiving a letter from Robert, for Sir William had been right in saying that it might come in the *Pickle* which had brought Collingwood's dispatch.

When the letter arrived and they knew that Robert was safe, there were many tears, and Sir William gathered all the family, including Ben and Lucy with Cecily, into the drawing-room so that he could read them his son's account of the victory at Cape Trafalgar.

My dear family
By the time you receive this letter, you will have learned of ourgreat victory over the combined fleet at Cape Trafalgar and also of our great sorrow and distress at the death of Lord Nelson. I cannot describe the feelings of all aboard the Victory, *indeed of all who took part in the great battle; how we admired the brilliance and cunning of Lord Nelson in attacking with two columns and hitting at the enemy at its centre. Admiral Collingwood led the second column in the* Royal Sovereign. *We smashed through between the* Bucentaur *and the* Redoutable *and then got locked together with the latter. Whether the marksman on the mizzen mast of the* Redoutable *could actually see Lord Nelson on the quarter deck we will never know, but the fact remains that our commander wore his*

golden epaulettes and all his insignia as he always did, so he made a prime target. The sharpshooter was certainly near enough to strike the deadly blow. The ball from the musket lodged in Lord Nelson's spine and everyone knew that his end had come. I think that he knew it, too, for he died a few hours later.

Captain Hardy was with him and I was still on the quarter deck for the battle continued unabated even though every man of us was stunned with grief and most of the men crying and sobbing. He kept repeating 'I have done my duty' and his last words were 'Thank God I have done my duty,' I wonder if he ever knew that seventeen of the enemy ships had surrendered, with most of the others going back to Cadiz. They had thirty-three ships of the line to our twenty-seven so it was indeed a splendid victory, but at the awful price of losing a remarkable commander. I can imagine that all England will be mourning his loss.

I am so full of the battle that I almost forgot to tell you that you will never see your handsome son again! It is obvious from this letter that I am alive and well, but almost at the same time as the ball struck our dear commander, another shattered the rail just where I was standing and a splinter of wood sliced into my cheek. It was not a *bad wound and I kept going until the heat of the battle was over. The sawbones cleaned up the wound and put three stitches in, then he warned me that I would always have a scar; but that is a little price today, for I am in one piece.*

That is more than I can say for poor Maxwell as he is in a bad way having lost a leg beneath the knee; he bears the wound bravely, as you can imagine he would and it is beginning to heal. We had continuous gales and storms after the battle and some of the fleet lost a mast. There is no time to write more, I will give you a fuller account when I come home. This is coming in the schooner Pickle *and I hope it makes good speed.*

I hope to be with you soon.

Your loving son Robert

Robert's letter and Admiral Collingwood's dispatch from the scene of the victory at Cape Trafalgar were both read many, many times by every member of the household at Ferrers Court.

Lady Hadleigh was upset to hear of Robert's injury and she wept openly. 'Oh, poor Robert and Maxwell, too; and our great Lord Nelson gone, the whole country will be grieving.'

Carolyn tried to comfort her. 'We must remember it as a victory, Mama, and remember too, to give thanks that Robert is still alive and will be with us soon. Read his letter quietly to yourself and try and remember the courage of those who fought in the battle. Napoleon has been defeated at sea and it is what we all longed for.'

'You are a dear girl and I know how much it means to you that Robert is safe even if he is injured—Maxwell, too,' she added, as an afterthought, for she had private hopes of Carolyn and Maxwell Forbes.

Carolyn was stiff with anxiety at the thought of Maxwell losing his leg, and hoped and prayed that the wound would not become infected.

She was very grateful to have Cecily to talk to; little had been said about Maxwell since Cecily's arrival and the new governess was sensitively keen to learn about him and to wonder at Carolyn's obvious concern.

'You talked about this Maxwell once before,' Cecily said that evening. They were alone in the drawing-room as Lady Hadleigh had retired to bed with the headache and Lizzie was up in her room, her head deep in one of Mrs Radcliffe's romances. 'It was when you were telling me about Edwin's fall from grace.'

Carolyn nodded. 'He is a lieutenant on board the *Victory* and he helped Robert with his studies. Indeed, they have become very good friends and the last time they were at home, Maxwell stayed here with us. He was so good on the day of my wedding when Edwin did not appear, he went out of the church immediately to go to Edwin's house to see if perhaps he was ill.'

'You like him, Carolyn,' said Cecily quietly.

Carolyn nodded. 'Yes, I do like him very much. When he and Robert went off to rejoin the *Victory* at Portsmouth, I could not be sure of his safe return, but I did tell him that I would wait for him.' She paused and Cecily thought that she looked downcast. 'And now he has lost a leg in the battle so I suppose that it will be the end of his naval career.'

'I hope he comes here for your sake.'

'Why do you say that, Cecily?' asked Carolyn.

Cecily was forthright in her reply. 'I have the feeling that you would like to comfort him in his affliction. To be able to help him in the same way as he helped you when you needed it so badly.'

Carolyn agreed. 'Yes, you are right, but I must try not to dwell upon it too much.'

'I think I can sense a romance,' murmured Cecily. 'We will wait and see! I wonder how long it will be before the fleet reaches these shores? There will be great rejoicing when they arrive. It is such a great relief to us all to know that Napoleon's fleet has been defeated and that we will not have to face an invasion.'

'There is sadness, too, though. Many young

seamen and naval officers will not be coming back and I do not think that there is a person in this country who is not grieving at Lord Nelson's death.' Carolyn was very serious.

'He was a great man,' said Cecily, and they both knew that there was never a truer word spoken.

NINE

Lord Nelson's body reached England on 4 December and found a nation in mourning; a state funeral was planned for early in January. In between, the Hadleigh family celebrated Christmas and Robert's return home.

Lady Hadleigh was the first to greet him when he arrived and swooned away at the sight of the terrible red and livid scar across his cheek. Lizzie fetched the vinaigrette, while Carolyn put her arms around her brother and sobbed. 'You are home with us again, that is what matters most.'

He kissed her and hugged her tightly to him. 'Is Papa at home? No? I will see him soon. I must run upstairs and see the children.'

Before Carolyn had time to say a word, he had kissed her again and was running up the stairs to the schoolroom. Oh dear, she thought, he doesn't know about Miss Grimble

. . . I had better go after him, but Mama needs me; he will have to introduce himself to Cecily. She has heard me talk of him so often and she read his letter so she knows about his injury.

In the schoolroom there was enacting a touching scene.

Robert had burst into the room to be immediately seized upon by Ben and Lucy. He looked round for the familiar figure of Miss Grimble, but saw only the slight figure of a young lady dressed in a pretty grey dress; her dark curls were tied back and fastened with a black ribbon, her blue eyes staring at him.

'You must be Robert,' she whispered, seeing his naval uniform.

Robert, holding both Ben and Lucy to him, met the blue eyes.

'Who are you?' he asked abruptly.

She stood up and came to him, putting out her hand. Gentle fingers touched the cruel scar. 'Your poor face,' she said softly, then she smiled. 'But you are still handsome.'

Robert, thinking that he had never seen such a pretty girl, and deeply affected by her soft and caring touch, looked at her closely, then, feeling an emotion foreign to him, turned his attention to the children.

He lifted Benjamin up high and laughed at him. 'Ben, you must introduce us; who is this beautiful young lady?'

Ben, his feet on the ground once again, was very serious. 'This is our new governess, her name is Miss Burns, but Carolyn calls her Cecily. We like her. We liked Miss Grimble, but we like Miss Burns better because she goes riding with us. She knows lots of things that Miss Grimble did not know; she even told us all about how people lived hundreds—no, thousands—of years ago and they lived in caves and they didn't have knives to cut things, so they cut stones to make them sharp and put them on their spears when they went hunting and . . .'

Over Benjamin's head, Robert and Cecily's eyes met and this time their expressions held laughter.

'Miss Burns,' said Robert, 'I am charmed to meet you, but I do not understand anything. Where is Miss Grimble and however do you come to know about prehistoric times? We are only just beginning to understand such things.'

'I do not suppose that Carolyn had time to tell you,' Cecily replied. 'Miss Grimble had to retire—Carolyn will tell you about it. My father, who was an archaeological scholar, died recently and I had to find a post as governess to support myself. I was fortunate enough to come to Ferrers Court. That is all.'

Robert took the hand which had touched his face. 'I am more than pleased to make your acquaintance, but I must not stay as poor Mama swooned at the sight of me and I left her to Carolyn and Lizzie . . .'

The schoolroom door was opened and

Carolyn stood there, taking in the scene of Robert holding Cecily's hand and Cecily gazing at him as though she had fallen instantly in love.

Goodness gracious, thought Carolyn, are we going to have a romance on our hands? How very nice. I wonder I did not think of it, they are very well suited and Robert is still handsome in spite of the scar.

'You have met each other,' she said. 'Do I need to introduce you properly?'

Robert gave a laugh. 'Benjamin introduced us very nicely, thank you. But Miss Grimble? I hope she is not ill or anything.'

Carolyn shook her head. 'No, it is not that. Her brother-in-law died—you will recall him coming to take her to Ashford on her afternoon off—and she wanted to go and live with her sister. So now we have Cecily—I should say Miss Burns in front of the children—and we are very lucky. But, Robert, you must come to Mama. She will want to see that you are well in spite of your wound.'

'Yes, I was just that minute coming down. I will see you again soon.' He looked at Cecily. 'May I call you Cecily?' Cecily smiled. 'Not in the schoolroom, if you please, but in the evenings, Carolyn treats me as one of the family and I will see you in the drawing-room after dinner.'

'Splendid,' was all Robert said, and went downstairs with Carolyn, leaving a starry-eyed

Cecily in the schoolroom.

Lizzie had rung for tea for her mama and wine was brought for Robert. Lady Hadleigh sighed as she looked at him.

'It is not as bad as I first thought and you did warn us,' she said. 'It is so good to have you here, Robert. Your father will want to know all the details of the famous victory, but I am afraid that your mama does not understand naval things. But we are proud of you and thank God that you are safely home. Did Carolyn tell you about our dear Miss Grimble and the arrival of Cecily? I heard you come downstairs and guessed that you had been to the schoolroom. How did you like our new governess?'

Robert gave a grin. 'She is quite beautiful, Mama, and I am on the brink of losing my heart to her. But surely she is an unusual governess for she seems to be quite the lady.'

'She comes from a very good, old family,' replied Lady Hadleigh. 'Her father was a younger son and a scholar and she has been brought up very properly and very modestly by Mr Burns, her poor mother having died when Cecily was born. She found herself almost penniless and had no course but to become a governess. It is to our good fortune, for I consider her to be very suited to the task and the children love her.'

'So I understand. They told me that she goes riding with them. Is she allowed an afternoon off?'

They all laughed. 'Wednesday afternoon,' said Lady Hadleigh, 'just like Miss Grimble. But if you wish to ride with her on Saturday or Sunday then I hope you will, for Patty can look after the children, or they can come to the drawing-room for a treat.'

Carolyn knew that her mama was thinking of a romance between Robert and Cecily, just as she had done, but she said nothing. Her thoughts had turned in another direction, but she was glad that it was Lady Hadleigh who asked the question.

'Robert, what about poor Maxwell? He is not with you?'

Robert shook his head. 'No, he hired a carriage to take him straight to Maidstone. His parents are there now and will be glad to have him at home.'

'How is he?' ventured Carolyn.

'He is improving. He found it difficult about ship on the way home, but we had a day in Portsmouth and he managed to get hold of a crutch. He is not ill in himself, but it is a terrible shock to lose a leg; the wound has healed nicely according to the *Victory*'s doctor and I think the sea air has helped that. But he does get downcast for he feels his career is over. However, I think it cheered him to find how easy it was to get about once he had got used to the crutch. By the end of the day, he was swinging along at my side as though he had always had one leg. When I saw him off, he was in much better spirits and he made me promise to go over to Maidstone to see him before Christmas.' Robert looked at Carolyn. 'Would you like to come, too, Carolyn?'

'Maxwell may not wish to see me,' she said guardedly.

'Oh, I think he will. He often spoke of you and how he regretted having to leave you on the disastrous day of your wedding. Have you managed to forget the wicked Edwin? Did you receive any more news of him?' Robert asked, and tried to put the question tactfully, though he was certain that his sister's heart had not been in the match.

Carolyn nodded. 'Papa had a letter from the attorneys in Ashford, he will show it to you. As far as I know, the Bow Street Runners are still after Edwin in London so he will probably end up in the Marshalsea.'

'You sound hard, Carolyn,' observed her brother.

'Edwin was wicked, Robert; he deceived us all and he deserves to be punished. I do not think of him. But, Robert, I am grateful to Maxwell for the way he helped us on that terrible day. I shall never forget his kindness.'

'Then you can come to Maidstone one day soon and thank him properly,' decided Robert. 'I know that Maxwell will be glad to see you . . . I do believe that you are flushing, Carolyn. Does Maxwell mean something special to you?'

Carolyn *had* felt herself flushing at the thought of seeing Maxwell again and with the sudden memory of their kisses. She ignored Robert's question.

'If you think that Maxwell would be pleased to see me then I will willingly come to Maidstone with you,' she told him.

The visit to Maidstone was made a week later on a crisp and bright morning just before Christmas; Robert decided to travel in the carriage as he thought that Carolyn would feel the cold in the gig. The road between Ashford and Maidstone was a good one and, as the Forbes's family house was in the village of Bearsted on the Ashford side of the town, the journey did not seem to be a long one.

Carolyn was feeling somewhat apprehensive, wondering to herself what to expect when she saw Maxwell again.

The Forbes's family seat was in Scotland, but as Maxwell's mother was a Kentish girl, the year had always been divided between the two homes and the colder months were spent in the south.

Woolstone House was not old, but it was gracious, having been built some fifty years before at the beginning of the reign of the present king.

Robert and Carolyn were admitted by a polite maidservant and they were not left standing in the entrance hall for more than a

141

second. Carolyn heard a tap of wood on the polished floor and suddenly a smiling Maxwell swung into view, not in the least slowed down by the loss of a leg.

But he looked older; pain had etched lines into his forehead and his face was thinner. Carolyn took one look at him and knew she loved him, but she had no time to ponder on the flash of emotion for Maxwell was before her, taking her hand and apologizing that his other arm was in use so he could not hug her to him as he wanted to.

'Carolyn, it is so good of you to come and visit the invalid,' he said cheerfully.

She smiled happily. 'You do not look invalidish to me, Maxwell, I am astonished at your speed with the crutch. Is your leg very painful?'

'Sometimes,' he admitted. 'Mostly at night, but as soon as the wound has healed properly, the doctors in London are going to fit me up with a wooden leg, so I won't have the nuisance of the crutch and I will be able to take you into my arms properly!' He turned to Robert. 'You look well, Robert, I think the scar is going to add to your attractions. Thank you for bringing Carolyn. Now come into the drawing-room and meet my mother and father.'

They spent a pleasant day and returned to Ashford before nightfall.

During the day, Carolyn had begun to think

that she was not going to be with Maxwell on her own; for this she was partly thankful as she was afraid of betraying new found feelings which had grown and deepened as the day had passed and she realized how bravely and cheerfully Maxwell was facing his disability.

Just before they prepared to go home, Maxwell sat himself at Carolyn's side on the sofa; she noticed that he managed to do so without any awkwardness.

'Come into the conservatory before you go, Carolyn. I have not seen you on your own the whole day and I want to make certain that you are not grieving over the dishonest Edwin.'

The Forbes's house had a small glass conservatory at the back of the house, full of palms and ferns. It was green and cool. Maxwell had told Carolyn to put on her pelisse and she was not cold as they walked around. At his closeness, she felt an unexpected quiver of excitement. I must not show how I feel, she thought, with an inward warning to herself.

Inside the door was a seat which was used in the warmer months, but Maxwell bade her sit down and placed himself beside her. 'Do you realize, my dear Carolyn,' he said quietly, 'that the last time I saw you was on the wedding day which never was? Did you recover from the shock of it all?'

'Yes, thank you, Maxwell. You helped me so much, I shall never forget it.'

'I would like to think that I could go on

helping you,' he said, 'but it was not meant to be.'

She found his words enigmatic, but did not press him further, deciding instead to speak of Robert.

'After you and Robert had gone, I went back to Canterbury with my aunt and uncle and my visit there helped me a lot. Has Robert spoken of Cecily to you?'

'Cecily? No, he has not mentioned a Cecily. Is it a romance?' he asked lightly.

'I hope so. She is a lovely girl. She was staying with my uncle. As she was left in poor straits she was looking for a post as a governess. When our own governess retired suddenly, we asked Cecily to come to us. She is no ordinary governess and the children love her.'

'And Robert? Does he love her, too?' Maxwell spoke lightly, but was keen to hear her reply.

'I cannot be sure,' replied Carolyn. 'I would like to think that he does, for I am sure of Cecily's feelings for him. But as they have known each other for only a few weeks, there is time. I thought I would ask you in case he had made mention of her to you.'

He grinned. 'Not a word. We still talk about the battle, both of us thankful that we are alive. We still marvel at Lord Nelson's tactics, attacking in two columns. I shall never forget the sight of the whole fleet lined up like that with the *Victory* leading our division and Collingwood leading the other in the *Royal Sovereign.* The enemy seemed to be in confusion, struggling like a forest of leaves across five miles of sea. Did you hear that Admiral Collingwood has taken Lord Nelson's command in the Mediterranean?'

Carolyn nodded, wondering at the same time if Maxwell would ever be able to go back to sea again; she did not like to make mention of it.

He answered for her. 'My naval days are over, dear Carolyn. I am lucky to be alive, but I am uncertain of what the future holds for me. I would like to be able to say certain things to you, but I cannot. I trust that you will find a better gentleman than Mr Edwin Baillie and I wish everything of the best for you. You do understand, don't you?'

Carolyn felt as though she was going to cry. Tears pricked at the back of her eyes and she tried to blink them away.

But Maxwell had been watching her and leaned towards her. 'Not tears, Carolyn. Do not weep for me, I am not worth it. Let me kiss them away.'

She steeled herself against his closeness, his touch, knowing that she might give herself away. She felt firm lips touch eyes which were not wet, and cheeks which felt as though they were on fire; then those same lips touched hers. As at their previous parting, the soft pressure was gentle with no hint of passion; then, also as at that last meeting in the shrubbery, he got up and walked away, swiftly swinging his injured leg. She followed to join the others in the drawing-room and shortly Robert was with her in the carriage on their way back to Ashford.

Robert was curious and did not hide his curiosity. 'Why did Maxwell take you apart, Carolyn. Did he propose to you?'

Her laugh was an attempt to hide her emotion. 'No, quite the opposite, Robert. He was trying to tell me that he could not ask me to marry him: his future is too uncertain. He says that his naval days are over.'

Robert was thoughtful; he had entertained hopes of Maxwell and his sister, whom he thought had been drawn to each other even when Carolyn was planning to marry Edwin. That had gone wrong and he had hoped that Carolyn would turn to Maxwell. He knew that his friend loved his sister, but he could understand the problems facing him. But there was no harm in speaking the truth.

'Do you love him?' he asked quietly.

'Yes, I do.'

It was a short reply and Robert said no more. He started to talk about Cecily Burns and Carolyn gave a sigh of relief as they reached safer ground.

Christmas was soon upon them and the festive season that year had an air of joy about

146

it, for it was the first time for many years that England had not been under threat from across the Channel. Although news had come of Napoleon's victory at the Battle of Austerlitz, that Christmas, Moravia seemed a long way away.

Uncle George Hadleigh had invited Cecily back to them for the Christmas period, but by this time, she had become one of the family at Ferrers Court and they begged her to stay. Robert added his voice to the persuasions keenly, for he and Cecily had become very good friends and rode out together on her afternoon off.

The Wednesday before Christmas that year was not a fine one and the two of them decided to ride up to the Downs rather than to the more solemn Marsh for which neither of them shared Carolyn's passion.

They galloped up a gentle slope towards a copse above Hastingleigh and when they reached the sparse shelter, both of them were laughing. Robert got there first to help Cecily to slide off her horse's back and into his arms. There was an excitement between the two of them which had been building up since their first meeting a few weeks before.

Robert was not going to let her go. 'I am going to kiss you, Cecily,' he said and, looking up at him, she realized that he was very serious. She could not pull away from him without a struggle, nor did she wish to, for she was where she felt she wanted to be for the rest of her life.

But she reached up and kissed his cheek just on the spot where his scar was fading.

'You do not mind if I am scarred, Cecily?' he asked her.

'I honour you for it,' she replied. 'It reminds me that you were in that great battle at Cape Trafalgar and that you came safely through it.'

'When I came home, you were here,' he said with a smile. For a moment, he had forgotten the kiss.

'Yes, I shall never forget the expression on your face when you walked into the schoolroom and found that Miss Grimble had been replaced by me! I will make a confession, Robert, and you will think me very forward.'

'What is that?' he asked her, knowing what the answer was going to be.

'I fell in love with you then,' she said softly.

'And I with you. Oh, my dear, sweet Cecily, I love you so much.'

Robert did kiss her then. She was gathered even closer and his lips found hers in a long and loving kiss.

He spoke at last. 'We love each other but I do not know if I can ask you to marry me.'

Cecily was startled. 'Whatever do you mean?'

'I am a naval man, Cecily, I can be away for months, even a year at a time. How can I ask a wife to wait that long at home?'

'It is easy,' she said, and there was mischief in her voice. 'I will have our children for company.'

Robert thought he was not easily shocked, but then, this was his Cecily. He should know her by now, or was he only just beginning to know her?

'Cecily Burns! Young ladies are not supposed to speak of such things. What shall I do with you?'

'Kiss me again.'

It was an even longer kiss this time and both of them knew happiness.

'Does it mean that you will accept my proposal if I ask you to marry me?' he asked her.

'Yes, please, Robert, I would like to marry you very much, it would make me so happy.'

'One day,' he told her, 'I might be a commander or even a post captain.'

'I would marry you if you were still a midshipman,' she said with a laugh.

'Those days are in the past! Kiss me once more, then we will ride back and tell the family at home.'

Their news caused both excitement and joy at Ferrers Court, but Lady Hadleigh suddenly gave a wail.

'I shall lose my governess again.'

It was Robert who spoke. 'Mama, I have explained to Cecily that I will be away much of the time, so why don't we make our home here

149

with you until Ben and Lucy are old enough not to need a governess.' He turned to Cecily. 'Would you be willing to be both wife and governess, my love?'

Cecily was very pleased with the idea. 'It does mean that I would not be on my own and I do love you all.'

Her words solved all the problems and the engagement between the two of them was celebrated on Christmas Day amid much laughter and rejoicing.

If Carolyn had a little ache in her heart for Maxwell, she did not show it.

TEN

Before the new year of 1806 had dawned, the family at Ferrers Court had made elaborate preparations for their removal to the North Audley Street House in London. Benjamin and Lucy were to be included in the party, much to their excitement and to the pleasure of Robert and Cecily.

Along with thousands of other families, they were repairing to the capital to be in time for the state funeral procession of Lord Nelson which was to take place on 9 January.

With the new year upon them, Carolyn was making resolutions to try and put all thoughts of Maxwell Forbes from her mind, but she was soon to be thwarted.

The journey into London passed without incident, Sir William having hired an extra carriage for the servants and the luggage. At North Audley Street, they soon settled in to wait for the big day; Ben and Lucy were excitable so Robert and Cecily kept themselves busy by taking the children to Hyde Park and to the great circus at Astley's Amphitheatre. Another favourite outing was to see the wild beasts in the Tower. Lizzie went with them on these occasions much to her delight.

Carolyn found herself at a loss; strangely, she missed Edwin for the first time, for she had no escort and contented herself by strolling through Hyde Park or down to the Burlington Arcade with her mama.

Her mopish mood was suddenly dispelled by the arrival at the house of Maxwell.

Carolyn was upstairs in the drawing-room when she heard the commotion of his arrival at the front door; there was no mistaking his cheerful voice. But she panicked; he would not be able to get up the stairs and she would have to take him into the dining-room.

She was the only one of the family at home at that moment, Sir William having taken Lady Hadleigh on a drive to Richmond; Robert and Cecily, with Lizzie and the children had gone on yet another visit to the Tower of London.

Carolyn hurried down the stairs and wondered if she was right in her senses when she saw the visitor; she was so certain it had been Maxwell's voice.

Standing in the small entrance hall at the foot of the stairs was a gentleman dressed in the first stare of fashion; white breeches with Hessians, a tight fitting knee-length coat of a deep gold, the colour of which was matched in the elegant waistcoat, and an elaborate neckcloth of pure white linen.

Carolyn paused half-way down the stairs. Was it Maxwell? She had only ever seen him in his naval uniform; or could it possibly be the brother he had spoken of, come down from Scotland for the funeral procession?

'Hello, my dear Carolyn,' said the stranger, but there was no mistaking Maxwell's voice.

'But . . . but . . .' Her voice failed her.

'I thought that you would be pleased to see me,' he said.

She took another step. 'Is it really you, Maxwell?'

'Of course it is me!' He gave a laugh and then added in a teasing voice, 'Were you expecting another gentleman? Have I been replaced in your affections?'

Carolyn walked down the rest of the stairs to stand at his side. 'No, of course not,' she said in a rather cross voice. 'But what has happened? Where is your crutch? How is your leg?'

'Wooden,' he stated. 'The best wooden leg the London doctors could make. We have stuffed my boot so that the leg fits in, my knee is still quite good, of course. I limp, but I am becoming accustomed to it. Only one problem, so far.'

'What is that?' she asked.

'I have not managed to get on a horse, but it will come in good time. Are you going to welcome me?'

Carolyn smiled then and she reached up and kissed his cheek shyly; it was to show her pleasure, but it was not enough for Maxwell.

He took her in his arms and kissed her. The kiss was not gentle and its persistence showed his gladness and relief at his transformed self. Carolyn could sense the love he had hinted at.

'Maxwell,' she said breathlessly, as she drew away from him. 'I am the only one at home. Can you manage the stairs to the drawing-room?'

'I am practising on stairs,' he told her. 'It is a little awkward, but it gets easier every day. Did you say that you were on your own? That sounds promising. Do you think we could try your bedroom rather than the drawing-room?'

'Maxwell,' she shrieked. 'How dare you? That was not the remark of a gentleman. I still cannot believe it is really you. The old Maxwell would never have dared to suggest or even mention such a thing.'

He laughed. 'It was when I threw away the crutch and got used to my new leg. I felt a different person. I suddenly realized that I was not as badly injured as I had believed when it was all so painful. I feel as though a new Maxwell Forbes has been born!' He took her by the arm. 'I am teasing you, my dear, it is very shocking of me. Let me try the stairs and I will settle for the drawing-room.'

'I had not expected to find you in London, Maxwell.'

'My parents decided to come for the great occasion, so I thought I might as well come with them. I guessed that you would be here.'

'Where are you staying?'

'We are in our house in Brook Street,' he told her.

'But that is only just round the corner from here.'

He smiled. 'Yes, I have walked here, I am practising with my new leg! I did not know if I would find you in, but I have been lucky. Would you like to walk in the park with me?'

'It is too far for you,' she replied, secretly delighted.

'No, I must get used to it. The doctors said to walk as much as possible, not to be afraid of the thing. While I am in London, I am to have an interview with Lord Barham.'

'Lord Barham?' she echoed. 'He is the First Lord of the Admiralty, is he not? I have seen his name in *The Times*. I think that Mr Pitt has depended upon him.'

'Yes, you are quite right, Carolyn. He is an old friend of my father who has suggested that

I might try the Admiralty Office now that I cannot return to sea. I am not sure that I would like to be deskbound, or that I would wish to live in London, but I have to consider my future. The alternative is to go up to Scotland and to help my brother with the Scottish estate, but the two of us have never dealt particularly well together and to be honest with you, I do not like his wife!' He gave a short laugh and she thought he was going to say more about his future intentions. She did not seem to have a part in them, she thought ruefully.

'Now tell me how young Robert is. I received a letter from him to say that he had become engaged to the Cecily you mentioned to me. Do you approve?'

Carolyn was enthusiastic. 'We are all very happy about it. Please stay a little while if you can, Maxwell; they have both of them been very good to take Ben and Lucy about and Lizzie goes with them. The wild beasts in the Tower are the favourite attraction and they are there again today, but I expect them back very shortly.'

'We will go for a walk first and I will see them on our return. Find a warm pelisse, Carolyn, for the wind is quite chill today. You are sure you will not mind being seen with a gentleman who limps?'

She could not tell if he was serious or if it really did bother him that he was handsomely dressed, but not able to walk without a limp.

'I will be proud to be seen with you, Maxwell, you are one of the nation's heroes.'

They reached Hyde Park and admired the horses and the extravagant phaetons and curricles.

'If I lived in London, I would have a phaeton and drive it in the park,' avowed Carolyn.

He glanced at her quickly. 'Do you mean that you would not object to living in London?' he asked her.

She looked up at him, but could not read his meaning; she would have to be honest.

'I would hate it; I am a country girl. Who could live in a city after being brought up in the wild vastness of the Marsh? On the other hand, I suppose it is possible to adapt oneself. That is what you have had to do, Maxwell. It cannot be easy for you after all those years at sea.'

'I am pensioned off,' he said, making a joke of it. 'I will have to make the most of my life if only I can decide what to do for the best. I am not even sure if I will be able to ride again, or not. Life throws these hurdles at us and we have to try and climb over them.'

'I suppose Edwin was a hurdle,' mused Carolyn. 'I think I have climbed that one.'

They both laughed and turned to walk back to North Audley Street and to a riotous time in which Ben and Lucy tried to describe the animals they had seen; Maxwell showed them his new leg. Then he was introduced to Cecily and took an immediate liking to her; congratulations and wine and cake followed until it was time for Maxwell to return to Brook Street for dinner. They were unable to persuade him to stay to dinner with them, but made arrangements to meet on the day of the funeral procession.

In between, Maxwell would be occupied with forming a new career for himself and Carolyn was left with the sad feeling that she was not to be part of it.

On Thursday 9 January, 1806, the day of the great procession for Lord Nelson's state funeral, by three o' clock in the morning, vast throngs were making their way from every direction into the heart of London.

All street traffic had been stopped along the route of the procession which was to start at Admiralty Arch and proceed to St Paul's Cathedral; it had been Lord Nelson's wish to be buried in the crypt of the cathedral and not in Westminster Abbey. The route lay through Charing Cross, then along the Strand to Fleet Street and Ludgate Hill.

At North Audley Street, the scene was chaotic though Sir William was doing his best to achieve some sense of order into his excited family.

The excitement was made even more intense because Robert was to be one of the seamen from the *Victory* to walk in the procession; there were forty-eight of them, all in ordinary dress with black neckerchiefs, black stockings and black crape on their hats. Robert had left the house in the small hours of the morning.

As no carriages were allowed, Sir William had decided to walk with Lady Hadleigh, Lizzie and Cecily and the children, together with the servants, as far as Charing Cross to watch the procession as it started off from the Admiralty.

Maxwell had promised to come for Carolyn and he was at the house before dawn, just as drums beat through every quarter of the city summoning the Volunteer Corps who were to line the route every step of the way from Admiralty Arch to St Paul's.

Maxwell joined the family in the dining-room for an early breakfast and Sir William told them all to eat heartily for it would be a long day.

'Do you want to stay with your family, Carolyn?' Maxwell asked her.

'If I am to be with you, Maxwell, I would like to try and get near to St Paul's; Ludgate Hill maybe. Are you agreeable and can you walk that far?' She asked the question apologetically.

'I can walk any distance as long as I am with you,' he teased her. 'I know that you would want to be in a good position to see Robert.

158

Ludgate Hill it shall be. We should set off straight away as the city is fast filling up. Wear your warmest pelisse, Carolyn, and a muff and bonnet for there is a real January chill out of doors.'

But walking did not prove to be easy in the crush of people; it was still not quite light and the dim street lights along the cobblestoned roads cast but a faint glow over the clusters of dark figures who were huddling together to keep warm in the pervading winter damp and cold.

It took Maxwell and Carolyn nearly two hours to reach Ludgate Hill, but once they were in sight of St Paul's, Carolyn was happy to squeeze into a space in the crowd.

They knew the sequence of the procession for Maxwell had made all the enquiries.

Lord Nelson's body had been lying in state in the Painted Hall of the Greenwich Hospital from 5 January to the 7th and on the day of the funeral procession, the Thames was cleared for the State barges taking part in the journey up the river.

During that morning, all taking part had been gathering at St James's Park, the procession being due to leave Admiralty Arch at noon.

It *was* cold and Carolyn was glad of Maxwell's protective arm around her, formality having been dispensed with on such an occasion, for nothing like it had ever been seen in London before.

As the first sounds of the procession came up the hill, every hat in the crowd was taken off, every sound was hushed. Carolyn found herself whispering.

'Will you tell me who everyone is, Maxwell?'

His hand tightened on her waist. 'I will if I can. I don't know it all, you must realize that, but the procession is led by General Dundas and the chief mourner is Sir Peter Parker. All the mourning carriages will be draped in black.'

They soon got used to the sound of the drums and fifes which set the pace and the only other sound was of the horses' hoofs and the wheels of the carriages on the cobbles.

Carolyn stood in rigid solemnity and she felt it echoed in all those around her.

Maxwell kept up a steady whisper. 'Those are the representatives of the Colleges of Arms and here are some of the pensioners from the Greenwich Naval Hospital and . . . oh, Carolyn, this is the moment you have been waiting for, the sailors and marines from the *Victory* . . . stand still, my dear.'

Carolyn could pick out Robert and was proud; tall and determined, sad and respectful, his scar showing vividly under the black crape of his hat.

'I am going to cry, Maxwell,' she said, and she felt the tears come into her eyes.

'I am holding you, Carolyn, be proud of

him.'

'He has come back, Lord Nelson did not,' she said against his chest.

'Lord Nelson died saving his country; there must be a thanksgiving behind our sadness. Try and watch the rest of the procession, Carolyn.'

Drying her eyes with her muff, she looked up at him. 'But, Maxwell, why were you not picked to march in the procession?' she asked him.

He laughed. 'My dearest Carolyn, they would hardly have wanted a seaman with a limp to spoil the marching!'

She gave a cry. 'Oh, Maxwell, I am sorry, I am very sorry, I did not think. I don't notice it, you know—the limp, I mean—I suppose I have got used to it already. It was thoughtless of me, will you forgive me?'

'I will forgive you if you let me give you a kiss,' he teased her.

'But we are in a public place, you cannot . . . oh, Maxwell . . .' Her words were taken from her as he bent down and quickly touched her lips with his.

'Enough of kisses,' he told her. 'You are missing the Knights of the Bath—and here come the Treasurer and Steward of Lord Nelson's household, it is a very sad day for them. Then the Privy Councillors and all the nobility, I don't know one from another, I am afraid. But here is the Archbishop of

161

Canterbury . . . oh, the carriages are slowing . . . I wonder who is next.'

But it was Carolyn's turn to speak. 'Oh, surely that is the Prince of Wales, he looks very serious.'

'So he should,' said Maxwell, 'and he has all his brothers with him. They are all dukes, but I cannot remember their names . . . oh, that is Captain Robert Moorsom of the *Revenge*, I expect the other captains are still in the Mediterranean . . . and look, Carolyn, all Lord Nelson's accoutrements, I think you call them, his gauntlet and spurs and there is his coronet on a black cushion, too. Everything is black today.'

There was a lull in the procession and Maxwell thought he knew the reason. 'It must be nearly time for the hearse for here are the coaches with the six admirals who are to bear the canopy over the coffin in the cathedral . . . yes, here is the hearse now and look, the Grenadier Guards are going into the churchyard of St Paul's and lining the space to the door.'

Carolyn tugged at his arm. 'Maxwell . . . look . . . oh, I should not be speaking, but the hearse, it is in the shape of the *Victory*, oh, I am going to cry again.'

'Hush, hush, Carolyn, bow your head or something.'

As the last of the long procession disappeared into the cathedral and all the

162

carriages found places to wait, the crowds of people began to drift slowly away though there were many who were prepared to wait to see the solemn day through to the end.

'What shall we do, Maxwell?' asked Carolyn. The excitement over, she realized that she was both cold and hungry; in fact, they had stood still for so long that she felt stiff with the cold and longed to be at home.

'I expect you are cold and hungry, my dear,' said Maxwell echoing her thoughts.

'Yes, I am,' she told him.

He looked at her in some concern for her face was unusually white. 'I don't think that you are in any state to walk back to North Audley Street,' he said. 'I will take you to a respectable hotel I know of; it is just off the Strand and not far away. We will have an early dinner and that will put some heart into you. The day has been quite a strain for everyone.'

'I would not like to have missed it, though. Thank you for bringing me, Maxwell. I did prefer being up here near St Paul's.'

They walked back to the Strand in silence and when they reached the hotel, Carolyn was relieved to find many ladies and gentlemen there. Indeed there were whole families, all enjoying a good dinner.

There was much talk of Lord Nelson and the Battle at Cape Trafalgar in the hotel dining-room that day, but as their meal drew to an end, Carolyn saw that Maxwell seemed to be struggling to say something more personal to her.

'Carolyn, it has been an honour to be with you for the state funeral of our great commander and I shall not forget the day in a hurry. But I feel I must end it on a more personal note as it looks as though I am forced to remain in London. I have a very high regard for you, Carolyn, but I will be desk-bound in a miserable way. You have told me that you would hate to live in London so I cannot consider asking you to marry me.'

'But, Maxwell—'

'No, I will not have arguments. My mind is made up. I cannot ask a young lady who is accustomed to riding wild on Romney Marsh every day, to be my wife and have to endure a life in London.'

'But, Maxwell, you are not giving me a chance to say anything.'

'There is nothing more to say . . . where are you going?'

The question came sharply as Carolyn had jumped up and started to walk away from the table in search of her pelisse. 'I am going to walk back to North Audley Street.'

'You will do nothing of the kind. A lady cannot walk alone on such a day as this, the streets are still crowded.'

'I can, Mr Maxwell Forbes.'

'I must come with you, Carolyn.'

'If you so please,' she retorted angrily.

Not a word was said between them as they walked through the crowds still milling about the streets.

At North Audley Street, Maxwell bade her a terse goodbye. 'I will not come in, I bid you good day.'

Carolyn entered the house, but said nothing to her family who were all talking excitedly about the funeral procession in the drawing-room, but went to her bedroom, threw herself on the bed and wept.

She loved Maxwell so much and now she had quarrelled with him.

ELEVEN

After the excitement of the London visit, and the quarrel with Maxwell, Carolyn's spirits were at a low ebb. For the first time in her life, even the Marsh did not console her. She did go and see Granny Harland as she knew that the old lady would want to hear all about Lord Nelson's funeral procession.

The air was very still that day and the Marsh seemed to have lost its life; it was very cold and even the sheep were huddled together for warmth. The waters of the dykes had lost their usual gleam because of their covering of thin ice. The ground was hard and Carolyn had to ride Trixie very carefully.

But she was pleased to be able to have a chat with Granny, who seemed to be philosophically certain that the lieutenant was the one for Carolyn. As she rode home over the Marsh, Carolyn was not so sure.

Two days later, Maxwell appeared. From the drawing-room window, Carolyn had seen a curricle being driven smartly up the drive and was curious as to its driver. As he drew nearer the house and she saw that it was Maxwell, she felt very flustered.

I don't want to see him, she told herself in a panic. He says that he cannot ask me to marry him if he is to be settled in London, but he did not consider my feelings. He would not let me say that I would live anywhere as long as I could be with him. He would not let me tell him that I loved him, but I suppose it was all my own fault for saying that I would hate living in London. Am I destined not to marry? First Edwin and now Maxwell.

Before the curricle had reached the end of the long drive, she had picked up a thick shawl of her mama's and was running to the stables. Cursing in an unladylike way because she would have to ride side-saddle, she led Trixie out of her stall, picked up a saddle and led the mare to the back of the house. She knew she would be out of sight of the stables where Maxwell would be stopping at any minute. As it happened, she was to learn later, her precaution had been unnecessary as Maxwell, in his haste to find her, had stopped outside the front door.

She was quick to saddle Trixie and was off through the orchard and on to the Marsh within minutes. The cold struck her straight away and she tried to wrap the thick shawl more tightly round her.

I will go over to Granny Harland's again, she was thinking, she will give me a hot drink and let me stay there until Maxwell has gone. I wonder what he can want when he has seen us so recently and is supposed to be in London having those interviews for the Admiralty Office.

The ground was harder than ever and she had to walk Trixie with care, and did not dare try a gallop which was what she was longing to do. That day, there was pale sunshine which held no warmth, but was enough to cast shadows of the bare willow and alder trees; even the sheep seemed brighter that day.

As she carefully rode the paths and tracks she knew so well, Carolyn felt the comfort of the Marsh return to her and her spirits rose. I belong here. I would be a different person anywhere else. How could I exist in a city the size of London? Maxwell knew. That is why he refused to ask me to marry him. But she felt confused; something is wrong, she was telling herself firmly. If I really loved Maxwell, I would follow him anywhere. To the north of Scotland, to the heart of London.

'Oh, Maxwell,' she cried, 'I will come to London with you. We could come and visit Mama at Ferrers Court, I would not have to lose the Marsh completely, or forever. How foolish I am, how very, very foolish.'

Unconsciously and in her distress, Carolyn urged Trixie on, forgetting the hard ground and the unevenness of the track she was on. Trixie stumbled and went down on her knees. Hardly knowing what was happening and still deep in thoughts of Maxwell, Carolyn went flying. Although a side-saddle was considered safer for ladies, it was very easy to slip from the saddle and fall to the ground if the horse faltered.

Carolyn would not have been so unfortunate if the ground had been soft, but she hit her head first—she had rushed out without hat, or bonnet—and then felt the pain of her ankle being twisted right over. She was stunned for a moment and lay still. Trixie, not damaged, was on her four legs again and nudging her nose against Carolyn's shoulder.

Carolyn seemed to come back to her senses from a great distance away. She tried to lift her head as she felt the mare close to her, but it was too difficult. The pain in her ankle was insistent and sharp, but at last, she sat up, patting Trixie's nose and speaking to the animal who was as close as a friend to her.

'Trix, Trix, I should not have hurried you, not on that ground. It is all my fault. Let me try and stand up.'

But standing proved impossible and she sank to the ground again, her hand to her head where she could feel a large bump. Oh dear, I have knocked myself out, as well. Now what shall I do? I am half-dazed and my foot will not bear my weight. What a pickle to be in and all in order to escape Mr Maxwell Forbes.

Whatever is the most sensible thing to do, she was asking herself? She stroked the mare's nose absently for it had given her the answer. Trixie will go home if I tell her to; we are not much more than a mile from the house. Then they will come and look for me. I know it might be Maxwell, but I cannot help that.

She sat up. 'Trixie. Home,' she commanded the horse.

Trixie nuzzled her again. 'No, Trixie. Home.'

The horse did not move and Carolyn became desperate. Then the thought came to her. I will pretend that I am dead, she thought. She lay down and kept very still, not moving when she felt Trixie's nose against her, but keeping herself stiff.

The ruse worked, for she heard Trixie give a long whinny and then came the sound of her hoofs on the dry, hard path as she returned in the direction they had come. Trixie knew the Marsh as well as Carolyn herself did.

After a few minutes, Carolyn felt it safe to sit up. She had to think of the best thing to do.

Of one thing she was certain, and that was that she could not possibly stay where she was; she was already feeling very cold and the pain in her ankle seemed to make it worse.

Where am I, was her first thought, and she looked around her, recognizing each stretch of marsh, each field, each dyke.

'That is Newchurch Dyke,' she said out loud to herself. 'I am nearer to Granny Harland than I am to Ferrers Court. I will crawl in that direction and Granny will put some salve on my ankle and bind it up for me. Then Joel can take me home in his cart when he comes in.' She picked up her riding whip and started to crawl forward, which did not prove to be easy. 'If Trixie arrives home without me, Robert will guess where I am, but I must keep trying.'

Painfully, with her knees becoming sore and her ankle hurting more every minute, she tried to make her way along the Newchurch Dyke. Every minute or so, she would stop and rest her head on the ground to try and regain her strength; then she became alarmed at how cold she was getting and she tried again.

As she lay there, trying to find some energy and by now feeling sick and dizzy from the blow to her head, she imagined that she could hear a voice in the distance. Thinking that she was becoming feverish and confused, she tried a few more crawling paces. Then the voice came again.

'Carolyn, Carolyn, answer me.'

It must be Robert, she thought; thank God, and she lay on the ground and cried.

'Carolyn, Carolyn.'

She raised her head with an effort. 'Here I am, Robert,' she tried to call out.

But it was not Robert who came over to her still figure, then lifted her into his arms. It was Maxwell.

*   *   *

At Ferrers Court, all was confusion. Maxwell had arrived and jumped down from his curricle outside the front door, raising the knocker impatiently. He was in a very keen mood to see Carolyn.

He was shown into the drawing-room by Patty who was puzzled to find the room empty.

'I thought Miss Carolyn were in here a minute ago, sir,' she said. 'I will go and find Lady Hadleigh. I expect she is with Cook, telling her about dinner.'

Lady Hadleigh came hurrying through to the drawing-room and greeted Maxwell with a broad smile. 'You have come to see Carolyn? I am so very pleased for I thought I had sensed a coolness between you before we left London.'

He spoke shortly. 'We quarrelled, Lady Hadleigh. I have come to see Carolyn to try and put things right between us. She is at home?'

Lady Hadleigh nodded. 'Yes, she was in

here a moment ago. Did she know that you had arrived?'

'No, I don't think so.'

'I will go and look for her, she is most probably in her bedroom. Robert and Cecily have taken the children out riding, I said that they could have a holiday from their lessons. Please sit down, Maxwell. I will go and find Carolyn and send her to you.'

Maxwell did not have to wait very long and when Lady Hadleigh came back, she looked puzzled.

'She is nowhere to be seen and I know that she has not gone out, for her pelisse and her riding-dress are in her bedroom, but she . . .' She was stopped short by a knock on the drawing-room door and the appearance of Mrs Bempton, who was Lady Hadleigh's cook.

'Lady Hadleigh, ma'am, I know as you'm looking for Miss Carolyn, and Barny, the stable lad, has just come to the back door to say that Miss Carolyn's Trixie is missing and her side-saddle gone, too. He says she must have saddled the mare herself, for he did not see none of it. She's gone, ma'am.'

Lady Hadleigh looked distressed and Maxwell looked grim.

'She must have seen me coming and run off — or ridden off, I should say—to avoid me,' he said tersely.

'I am very sorry, Maxwell, I cannot begin to understand it for it is a very cold morning and she has not even put on her warmest riding-dress . . . but look . . .'

She pointed to the chair by the fireplace which was usually regarded as hers.

'What is it, Lady Hadleigh?'

'My thick woollen shawl has disappeared; I can only think that Carolyn must have taken it.'

'I see.' Maxwell Forbes was rarely at a loss, but he was unused to a young lady riding off in haste in order to avoid him.

'I will ring for some wine for you, Maxwell. Please stay and wait until Carolyn returns.'

'Very well, I thank you,' he replied, and said no more.

Lady Hadleigh tried in vain to make conversation with her visitor and could not but hope that Carolyn would soon return. She had her own views on the friendship between her daughter and Maxwell; she also had hopes of it, but knew that the fact that Maxwell was considering the Admiralty Office must be an obstacle to a match between them.

Her thoughts were interrupted, not by anything Maxwell had said, but by hurrying footsteps from the direction of the kitchen and yet another appearance of Mrs Bempton, this time more upset than ever.

'Lady Hadleigh, Mr Maxwell . . . Barny is here again. He says that Trixie has returned on her own and no sign of Miss Carolyn . . . oh, please come quick.'

Maxwell jumped up and Mrs Bempton found the vinaigrette for her mistress, who had sunk back in her chair.

'I will go, ma'am, you stay here,' he told Lady Hadleigh hastily.

He hurried to the stables and found Trixie as Barny had said. He patted the mare's nose. 'Have you come to tell me something, Trixie?' he asked, as though he was talking to another person. Then he turned and gave sharp orders to Barny.

'Take the side-saddle off quickly and put the usual saddle on, I know that Miss Carolyn often rides astride. Trixie will probably take me in the right direction over the Marsh . . . I am certain that Carolyn will have gone to the Marsh,' he added, more to himself. Then a thought struck him as he remembered his leg . . . Be damned to it, I will manage somehow. 'You have a mounting block, Barny?' he asked.

'Here, sir,' said Barny. 'Shall I help you up?'

'No, damn you, I've got to do it some day.' He limped to the mounting block, and found to his astonishment that his wooden leg performed perfectly.

Carolyn's Trixie was a fine horse and bore him well. He trotted her through the gardens and orchard and then, as they reached the Marsh, he went more slowly, giving Trixie her head and calling Carolyn's name.

He was busy thinking at the same time; Carolyn will probably make for Granny

Harland whom she has mentioned so many times. That is in the direction of Newchurch, I do know that. But what about this Military Canal they are building? Maybe we are this side of it; Carolyn would know.

He had not reached the canal when Trixie suddenly slowed her pace. Maxwell called Carolyn's name again. Then he saw her lying near the dyke. She raised her head, and he heard her voice call feebly, 'Here I am, Robert.'

He reached her quickly and slid off Trixie's back and took Carolyn in his arms. She opened her eyes. 'Oh, it is you, Maxwell,' she said, and laid her head thankfully against his chest.

'Carolyn,' he said urgently. 'I have brought some brandy in a flask. Please try and have a sip; it will warm you up for you are very cold. Are you injured?'

'Trixie came home?' Carolyn said. 'Oh, what a dear, clever horse she is.' She looked at him closely. 'But, Maxwell, you are riding, however did you manage?'

'I used the mounting block,' he said shortly. 'Never mind about Trixie: tell me what happened.'

With the warmth of Maxwell's body close to her and the glow from the brandy, Carolyn began to recover.

'Maxwell, I did not want to see you . . .' she started to say.

'I know that. You thought I had come to persuade you to live in London if we were to marry. But we are not going to talk about it now, tell me if you are injured. Were you on your way to Granny Harland?'

'Yes, I was and the ground was hard and I was not thinking properly. I hurried poor Trixie and she went down on her knees. Is she all right? Yes, she must be if you are riding her. I was thrown and hit my head and I think that I was stunned for a moment. When I came to, I tried to stand up and my ankle would not let me. I could not walk, I could not even get up on Trixie.'

'So you sent her home?'

'Yes, the dear girl, what sense they have, Maxwell,' she said to him.

'Never mind about Trixie, tell me what you were going to do.'

'I was going to try and crawl to Granny Harland's, but it was so difficult. I soon got exhausted and I think I was about to go into a swoon. Then I heard your voice. I thought it was Robert at first. What shall we do now, Maxwell?' she said uncertainly.

'How near are we to Granny Harland's?' he asked her.

'It is less than a mile: her cottage is on this side of the village,' she replied.

'What were you going to do if I had not come?' was his next question and she thought he sounded stern.

'Well, I worked it out that if I wasn't found, I would get to Granny's somehow and she would bind up my ankle and perhaps give me some hot milk and then, when her grandson, Joel, came home, I would ask him to take me back to Ferrers Court in his cart. I am afraid that I have been a lot of bother.' Carolyn felt apologetic, but so, so much better to have Maxwell with her.

'So you have, young lady. We will get you up on Trixie and I will ride behind you and we *will* go to Granny Harland's, for I think you need the hot drink. I would very much like to meet the good woman, in any case.'

They somehow managed between them both to get on to Trixie and the mare did not seem to object to her two riders. They set off carefully towards the cottage.

'Miss Car'lyn, whatever next?' exclaimed Granny Harland.

'Oh, Granny, I came off Trixie and the dear horse went all the way back to Ferrers Court and Maxwell came to find me. I have hurt my ankle. Granny, this is Mr Maxwell Forbes. He was a lieutenant on the *Victory* with Robert, but he was badly injured in the battle at Cape Trafalgar and he has a wooden leg. He thought he would not be able to ride again, but he managed to get up on Trixie and he came to my rescue. It was over near Newchurch Dyke. I was on my way to see you.'

'My soul, what a tale. You come in, sir, and

I'm very pleased to meet you. I will fetch you some ale and hot up some milk for Miss Car'lyn.'

Maxwell helped Carolyn from Trixie and picked her up, then carried her into Granny Harland's warm kitchen.

'I will bind up your foot for you, Miss Car'lyn, but I am not having you staying long for your poor mama will be in a fuss over you. Mr Maxwell, sir, can I ask you if you are a gentleman who likes the Marsh?'

Carolyn knew what lay behind the question and hid a smile.

But Maxwell was able to answer truthfully. 'My home is in Bearsted near Maidstone, Granny Harland, but I have known Romney Marsh from a child. There is something bewitching about the Marsh, I have always thought.'

Granny beamed. 'That's all right then. Miss Car'lyn will tell you why I asked. I think as things is going right at last.'

She would say no more, bound up the injured foot and Carolyn managed to limp to the patiently waiting Trixie. Up in front of Maxwell once again, she thanked Granny Harland and listened to the parting words with a sense of happiness.

'God bless 'ee, Miss Car'lyn, and you, too, Mr Maxwell and I think as it's heart not head this time.'

They rode off and Maxwell whispered in

178

Carolyn's ear. 'Whatever did she mean by those last words?'

'Maybe I will tell you one day, Maxwell,' was all that Carolyn would say.

Back at Ferrers Court, there were tears and kisses and a lot of fuss, then they all sat down to a luncheon in the dining-room.

As they rose from the table, Maxwell took Carolyn's arm and drew her to one side. 'You have not asked me why I came to see you today,' he said to her.

'I supposed it was to tell me that you had obtained a post with the Admiralty,' she said, then made herself tell him of her thoughts. 'But, Maxwell, when I was riding across the Marsh, I was thinking that I should not have refused to live in London if you had wanted it.'

'You really mean that, Carolyn?' There was a quizzical note in his question.

'Yes, Maxwell, I do,' she replied, and she knew she was being sincere and perhaps giving away her feelings.

'It tells me a lot, Carolyn. Now I will tell you why I have come. Do you think we could borrow your father's gig?'

'The gig? Whatever do we want with the gig?' she asked, curious at the request.

'I want to take you somewhere. Do you think that your foot would permit a short outing?'

She nodded. 'Yes, of course. It is feeling a lot easier since Granny bound it up for me.

She rubbed in some salve, as well. I think it is oil of wintergreen and it is very good stuff. It does smell rather strongly, but I quite like it.'

'I do not want to talk about oil of wintergreen, Carolyn, good though I know it to be,' he said. 'I want to take you somewhere.'

'Very well, Maxwell.' She was mystified, but interested to know his intention.

In the gig, he took the familiar lane into Ashford, but before they reached the town, Maxwell turned in to a long drive which led up to a handsome old farmhouse.

'But, Maxwell,' burst from Carolyn, 'this is Ridley House. What are we doing here?'

'I will tell you in a moment.'

She spoke crossly. 'You have some secret, or is it that you have brought me here to remind me of Edwin? I had hoped to erase him from my memory.'

They stopped at the front door and Carolyn looked around her. 'I always liked it and was sorry that I would not be living here,' she remarked. 'Though I have never been inside. It has lain empty for years. Edwin was to have it renovated for us while we were in Cornwall and I was going to choose the furniture and the furnishings.'

'You can still choose the furniture if you would like to, Carolyn.'

They were still sitting in the gig and she turned to him swiftly. 'Whatever do you mean by that remark?'

'I have bought Ridley House.'

'*You* have bought Ridley House?' she echoed. 'What are you saying, Maxwell?'

'You did not want to live in London, so I bought Ridley House and farm, together with the land attached to it. I will become a country gentleman.'

Carolyn found herself almost speechless. 'But, Maxwell, the Admiralty. What about your post with the Admiralty . . . and I told you that it was wrong of me to object to living in London . . . whatever are you about?'

'My dearest Carolyn, the Admiralty would not have me,' he told her seriously.

'Would not have you? Whatever next? But you told me that your father knew Lord Barham.' She could not believe what he was telling her.

'I did not go to Oxford, Carolyn. I was a midshipman at the age of fourteen and it was not enough that I was a lieutenant.'

'That is a disgrace . . .' she started to say. 'But does it mean that you will really come to live here in Ashford?'

'It does,' he replied. 'I think in the end that I had no wish to live in London either. I will manage the estate myself and will limp around it quite happily; we will not be paupers, my dear, I will have my naval pension.'

'*We*, Maxwell?' Carolyn was hearing words she wanted to hear and was daring to hope.

'Yes, did I forget to ask you to be my wife so

that we can make our home at Ridley House *and* still be near your Marsh?'

Carolyn thought she would swoon with the suddenness and happiness of it all.

'Have you an answer for me, then?' he asked somewhat abruptly.

'You forgot something,' she said.

'I have forgotten nothing, I have done it all for you.'

'But you forgot to tell me if you loved me.' Carolyn wondered what his reply would be.

His answer was to turn to her and slip his hands underneath her woollen shawl; they sought her body as his lips found hers.

Everything else forgotten, Carolyn thrilled to his touch as his seeking fingers found the soft skin under the bodice of her dress. 'Maxwell . . .' she breathed. 'You cannot.'

'Yes, I can,' he whispered. 'I love you and if I remember correctly, I told you that I loved you at our very first meeting. I also said that I would marry you. Does it mean that you love me, too? Will you marry me, Carolyn?' He lifted his head. 'Oh, and what was that parting remark of Granny Harland's? Something about head and heart.'

Carolyn gave a happy laugh. 'She told me that I was loving Edwin with my head; she knew as soon as she saw you that I had given my heart to you.'

'And have you?'

'Yes, Maxwell, you have my heart. I love you

and, yes, I would like to marry you.'

He kissed her again, swiftly, impatiently. 'Come along, we will look at our new home and then we must go and tell your mama. Do you think she will be pleased?'

'I know she will, especially if you promise not to abandon me on our wedding day,' she teased him.

His kiss told her all she wanted to know.